# DOCTOR ILLUMINATUS

The Alchemist's Son

# DOCTOR ILLUMINATUS

## Martin Booth

LITTLE, BROWN AND COMPANY

New York ↣ Boston

Little, Brown and Company

Time Warner Book Group
1271 Avenue of the Americas, New York, NY 10020
Visit our Web site at www.lb-kids.com

Library of Congress Cataloging-in-Publication Data

Booth, Martin.
  Doctor Illuminatus / by Martin Booth.
    p.   cm. — (The alchemist's son ; pt. I)
    Summary: Pip and her twin brother, Tim, awaken an achemist's
son from a centuries-long slumber when their family moves to an
old English country estate, and he enlists them in the fight against
an evil alchemist who seeks to create a homunculus.
    ISBN 0-316-15575-6
    [1. Alchemy — Fiction.   2. Magic — Fiction.   3. Brothers and
sisters — Fiction.   4. Twins — Fiction.   5. Adventure and
adventurers — Fiction.   6. England — Fiction.]   I. Title.
    II. Series: Booth, Martin. Alchemist's son ; pt. I.
    PZ7.B6468Do 2004
    [Fic] — dc22

                                              2004046540

First U.S. Edition published by Little, Brown & Company in 2004
First published in Great Britain by Puffin Books in 2003

10 9 8 7 6 5 4 3 2

Q–FF

Printed in the United States of America

The text was set in Bembo, and the display type is Tagliente.

For Lucy

# Contents

# The Alchemist's Son

## DOCTOR ILLUMINATUS

Martin Booth says: All the magic in *Dr. Illuminatus* is real: the chants, the herbs, the potions, and the equipment. The colophon [⚜] used in this book is an ancient alchemical symbol representing rebirth. It is also known as the *crux dissimulata* and was an early first-century Christian secret sign. The other [∞] is one of the many alchemical symbols for gold.

Alchemy, a curious blend of magic and science, was the chemistry of the Middle Ages. People who studied alchemy were called alchemists and they devoted their lives to the quest for the elixir of life and the means to turn ordinary metal, like iron, into gold. The third dream of alchemists was to create a homunculus — an artificial man made from dead material.

The Alchemist's Son, set in contemporary England but inextricably linked to its ancient, bloody past, explores this dark side of alchemy.

# One

# A Little Piece of History

Stuck to the heavy oak door was a fluorescent green Post-it Note upon which Pip's mother had written *Daughter's Room* with a broad blue felt-tip marker. Down the passageway, Pip could see other notes on other doors — *Son's Room*, *Master Bedroom*, *Guest Room 1* and *Bathroom*. Each one stood out in the semi-darkness, she thought, like a glowing, square green eye.

Lifting the iron latch, Pip stepped into her new bedroom. Compared to her last, it was huge, at least four meters square, with ancient mullioned windows set in sandstone. Two of the walls were lined with dark oak panels, and the ceiling was held up by massive wooden beams as black as if they had been charred in a fire. The floorboards were each of different widths, according to where they had been cut from the trunk of the tree. As she walked to the windows, they creaked.

"Well, what do you think of it so far?"

Pip turned around. Her father was standing in the doorway.

"It's . . ." Momentarily, she was lost for words.

"Is this a pretty spectacular house, or what?" her

father said for her. "And this," he looked around the empty room, "is a really stupendous bedroom."

Pip grinned. *Spectacular* was one of her father's favorite adjectives. *Stupendous* was the other.

"Your last one," her father continued, "was a rabbit hutch by comparison." He came to her side and gazed out of the window. "And to think that view's hardly changed in the last five hundred years. There's not a single tree out there that hasn't got a preservation order on it. I can't so much as prune a twig without local council permission."

Following his gaze, Pip took in the neat garden with its trim flowerbeds, smooth lawn and an ancient mulberry tree in the center, the curve of the gravel drive, down the center of which grew a strip of grass, and the pasture beyond with massive oak, elm and beech trees dotted about it. Farther off still was a river lined with pollarded willows.

"Once, the house was moated," her father went on. "See beyond the edge of the garden, where the ground dips? That was it. But in the eighteenth century, it was mostly filled in to make a ha-ha."

Pip, who was never quite sure when her father was being serious, gave him one of her disparaging looks and sarcastically replied, "Ha! Ha!"

"Really," he said, briefly pretending to be hurt. "It was a landscaping feature. A ha-ha is a grassy ditch, surrounding a house, that slopes down gently towards the building, but has a stone wall on the house side. The idea was to keep animals out of the gardens without a fence or hedge spoiling the view." He turned from the window and walked over to the door. "Your mother's put the kettle on. Tea and cake in ten minutes."

After he had gone, Pip unfolded the estate agent's leaflet she had in her pocket and, not for the first time that day, read the blurb printed on the front page beneath a color photo of the front elevation of the house.

*Rawne Barton*, she read, *situated in beautiful countryside three miles from the pretty market town of Brampton, offers a rare opportunity to purchase a Grade I-listed, landed-gentleman's country house set in thirty-two acres of pasture, formerly a deer park. Originally built in 1422, but extended over the following hundred years, the property comprises a spacious and superbly appointed six-bedroom family house with extensive period features including contemporary linen-fold paneling, beamed ceilings with carved features and magnificent fireplaces. Recent extensive modernization has been conducted to the highest standards and in complete keeping with the architectural and historical aspects of the house. A range of contemporary outbuildings includes a stable (restored and providing ample space for vehicles), a coach house and a malt-house (both in need of renovation: with planning permission).*

The photograph showed a building made partly of white wattle-and-daub and partly of brick with black timber beams built into the walls. Above the tiled roof stood two stacks of chimneys, added in the sixteenth century, made of the same sandstone as the window frames, but twisted in spirals like sticks of old-fashioned barley sugar.

"Do you know what *barton* means?"

Pip looked around to see her twin brother, Tim.

The knees of his jeans were grimy, his T-shirt was smudged with dirt and his brown hair looked as if it had been lightly powdered with flour.

"Try knocking," she said sharply.

"Door's already open," Tim responded, "and I'm not coming in." He slid to the floor, leaning against the doorpost. "It means a cow shed," he went on.

"No, it doesn't," Pip corrected him. "It means a farm owned by a landowner, not given to tenants. I looked it up." She ran her eye up and down her brother. "Why are you so grubby?"

Tim ignored her question.

"And you know what *Grade I-listed* means, don't you?" he continued. "It means we can't put up a satellite dish. Goodbye MTV and the Cartoon Channel."

"We can have one of those square ones in the attic," Pip said. "Grade I only means you can't alter the appearance of the house or destroy any historical features."

"They don't get such a good signal," Tim rejoined. "Besides, I've seen the attic. No chance. The rest of the house might have been modernized, but that hasn't. The cobwebs are like table-tennis nets."

"You've been up there?"

"There's a door at the end of the passage," Tim said. "I thought it was an airing cupboard, because it's got shelves and a copper water cylinder in it, but at the back there's an old paneled wall. One panel has a handle and slides sideways. It's a bit of a squeeze, which is probably why the builders didn't bother to go up there. Behind that, there're steps. The attic floor's boarded, but there aren't any rooms or anything, just a big space with a

4

little window at the end and a lot of beams, crud and cobwebs. And a dried-up dead bat."

One of the removal men appeared at the door carrying a large cardboard box with yet another Post-it Note taped to it.

"You the daughter?" he asked. "This your room?" He didn't wait for an answer but, checking the Post-it Note on the door against that on the box, entered, stepping over Tim and looking around. "Nice. Very nice. Quite a place your mum and dad've bought." He put the box down and glanced out of the window. "You know what you got here, don't you? You got a real little piece of history, you have."

The garden was protected on two sides by stone walls about two meters high, with rambling roses and honeysuckle trained up them. The flowerbeds were thick with bushes and low shrubs, most of which were perennials. Some had thick trunks and were plainly very old, having been carefully pruned over the years. Quite a number were in bloom and one, a jasmine with tiny white flowers like thin stars, was giving off a heavenly scent. The grass of the lawn was ankle deep and even now, in the early afternoon, damp.

Pip walked across the grass to the mulberry tree. It was positively ancient, leaning slightly to one side as if it were tired of supporting itself against the winds of time. Under the trunk was wedged a tough oak bar to hold it up. Like a mottled green umbrella, the tree spread its branches out from gnarled and twisting

boughs; the bark was hard, scaly and old. They reminded her of her grandfather's arthritic fingers.

Leaving its cool shade, Pip went over to the edge of
the ha-ha. It was just as her father had described it. The
ditch was filled with grass in which tall ox-eye daisies
and buttercups were growing. At one end, where the
soil looked to be damp up against the loose stone wall
retaining the garden, grew a clump of mugwort.

Pip knew her plants. She had once toyed with the
idea of going to horticultural college and becoming a
famous gardener, laying out the properties of film stars,
royalty and millionaires. Perhaps, she had dreamed, she
might end up as the head gardener for a palace or grand
stately home. She had never in her wildest imagination
thought that she might one day live in a smaller equivalent of such a house.

Making her way back towards the heavy oak door
that led from the garden to the hall, Pip suddenly noticed a strange bush. She had never seen anything like it
before. About two meters high and hidden against the
wall behind other shrubs, it had large, dark leaves that
looked as if they were made of velvet. Yet it was not
the leaves that caught her attention, but the flowers.
They were about fifteen centimeters long and hung
down under their own weight. The color of old ivory,
they were trumpet-shaped with frilled petals. The bush
held only three flowers, although the remains of several
more lay rotting on the ground beneath it. Five or six
buds were waiting to open.

Bending to a flower, Pip gently lifted it up. It was
surprisingly heavy. Clearly, few insects had visited it,
for the stamens were still covered in a green-tinged

pollen. She sniffed at it to see if it had a perfume. Instantly she felt giddy and, letting the flower go, reeled several steps back, her head spinning. The sensation passed quickly, but it left her puzzled. Surely, she thought, the flower could not have had that effect upon her. Somewhat more cautiously, she sniffed the flower again. It had a strange scent, a sort of mixture of sour milk and apple juice. No sooner had it hit her nostrils than, once more, she felt dizzy.

Determined to discover the identity of the plant, she continued on her way towards the house. Near the door, a buddleia was in full bloom, the tight spirals of deep mauve flowers attracting a small cloud of butterflies. Mixing with them were several honey- and bumblebees, dipping from flower to flower in their search for any nectar the butterflies had overlooked.

As Pip passed the buddleia, a butterfly settled on her arm. It was small and nondescript and yet, as it landed, it felt somehow heavy. Uniformly dull brown with several whitish markings along the edge of its wings, the only bright color it displayed was a single chalky yellow spot on each of its rear wings, near the abdomen. No sooner had it alighted than it dipped its head to the fine hairs on her arm and gave her a vicious sting. It was worse than a wasp, the pain as sharp as a red-hot hypodermic needle piercing her skin.

Instantly, Pip swept her hand down to swat it off, but the insect was too quick for her. With a speed she would never have expected from a delicate butterfly, it lifted off from her before she could squash it and, flying high, disappeared over the roof of the house.

Where it had landed on her skin was a circular red

7

weal the size of a coin, with a tiny pinprick of blood in the center.

"I'm sure you're mistaken, dear," her mother said as she cleaned the bite with disinfectant and warm water. "It was probably a wasp or a hornet or something."

"It was a butterfly," Pip insisted, desperately wanting to scratch her arm, which itched incessantly.

"Perhaps," her mother suggested, reaching into the bathroom cabinet for a tube of antiseptic cream, "it was a foreign butterfly. Maybe they bite. Blown here on the wind. It can happen, you know. Someone saw a hoopoe in Kent last year and that's a bird that only lives in Africa. And they say, with global warming, we'll soon have mosquitoes carrying malaria in England."

"Thanks, Mum," Pip retorted. "That's really comforting."

"Now leave it alone," her mother ordered, "and let the air get at it."

Yet, within an hour, all sign of the bite had completely vanished.

By dusk, Pip had more or less got her room sorted out: at least, her television and CD player were wired up and plugged in, her furniture was in the right position, her books were on her shelves in alphabetical order and the duvet was on her bed.

Although she was exhausted after all her efforts, she did not go to bed immediately, but opened one of the windows, leaning out as night fell over the pasture and trees. It was strange, she thought, how the light gradually faded and how, even after she could not make out their exact outlines, she could still somehow see the trees, as if their dark shapes had engraved themselves upon her eyes.

Yet there was something else even stranger. The whole landscape seemed utterly silent. The house the family had moved from had been in a large village and there was always some noise to be heard at night — the distant murmur of the pub and the far-off thunder of the wooden balls in the skittle alley at the back, a passing car or footsteps in the street. This house appeared to exist in a world without sound. Yet, the longer Pip stood still and listened, she began to pick up indistinct noises. The first was an unidentifiable, soft, persistent whisper, as if someone in the night were rubbing a piece of silk. The second, from the direction of the pasture, was a grunting cough, like an old man clearing his throat. The third, when it came, was close by and reminded her of the sound leaves make when they are burned.

Glancing up, she saw something materialize from the eaves just over her head. It was small and black, and — in an instant — was gone, only to be replaced by another, then another, and another. As each disappeared, a tiny breath touched her cheek as if a ghost were kissing her. The hair on the nape of her neck prickled. It was only then she remembered what Tim had found in the attic. These were not ghosts but bats coming out of their roost in the roof to hunt for midges over the pasture and the river, and which, she now realized, were the source of the sound of rubbed silk.

A few moments later, she saw something appear on

the top of the ha-ha. It had no definable shape and once in view remained quite still for as long as she stared at it. Then, just as she was about to turn her attention from it, it made the coughing sound and moved stealthily off. From its movement, she knew exactly what it was — a fox on its nocturnal prowl.

Closing the window, Pip crossed the room to her bed and slipped under the cover, lying on her back and staring at the beams of the ceiling. Even in the night, they cast lines of deeper darkness across the white plaster.

Bit by bit, as she had come to hear the noises in the night outside, Pip listened to those of the house settling down. With all the ancient wood used in its construction, it squeaked and clicked as the walls cooled after the hours of sunlight. It was, she thought, like a person going to sleep, easing their muscles after a day's work, their flesh twitching as their nerves relaxed.

Sometime in the early hours, just before dawn, Pip woke from a dream in which she was wandering through a strange house, getting lost in its labyrinth of long, twisting corridors and gloomy chambers where all the furniture stood about haphazardly. For a moment, she was afraid because she did not recognize her surroundings. It was as if her fantasy had become reality. Then, slowly, her fear subsided as she saw the tiny red light on her CD player, knew it for what it was and remembered she had, after months of being dragged with her brother from house viewing to house viewing by her parents, finally moved into one of them.

However, it was not, Pip soon realized, the scary dream that had woken her, but a noise in the wall behind her bed. At first, it was a slight and irregular scratching that she put down either to the bats returning to their roost before daylight or to mice scurrying about behind the paneling. Old houses, she reasoned, must have centuries of mouse holes gnawed, nibbled and dug in their walls. Yet, after a short while, the scratching ceased, replaced by a persistent, almost gentle, knocking. Going over the possibilities and admitting that the mice were hardly likely to be wearing boots or pick-axing a new run through the wall cavity, Pip reckoned it was caused by the central heating pipes warming up. When she looked at her alarm clock, she saw dawn was less than half an hour off and she knew her parents always liked to get up to a warm house.

The knocking soon became an irregular tapping and then, after about ten minutes, it stopped altogether. Pip gave it no further thought, pulled the cover up to her chin, turned over and went back to sleep.

The school secretary, a prim woman bearing her name — Mrs. Rigg — upon a label pinned to her substantial bosom, her hair scraped severely back into a bun, opened the door.

"Headmaster? I have Mr. and Mrs. Ledger here, with Philippa and Timothy."

Pip inwardly winced to hear her full name. Tim grinned at her and nudged her with his elbow.

As they were ushered in, the headmaster stepped from behind a large leather-topped desk, cluttered with papers and report forms, a telephone and a notebook computer.

"I'm Dr. Singall," the headmaster introduced himself. "Come in and, please, do sit down." He indicated a semicircle of comfortable chairs before him, perching himself informally on the corner of his desk.

Pip and Tim exchanged glances and looked around the room. One wall was covered with annual photographs of the staff and pupils, various triumphant sports teams and a portrait of a man in a gray suit shaking hands with the headmaster, the flourish of a signature in one corner. Printed on the picture mounting was *HRH Prince of Wales visits Bourne End Comprehensive School — July 2000*. Beside it was a map of the town and surrounding countryside, red felt-tip marker delineating the different areas served by the school buses, the routes picked out and numbered in blue. Another wall bore shelves of books and file boxes, and a glass-fronted cabinet.

"I understand from Mr. Bradley," the headmaster began, "who is in charge of admissions, that you have been given a tour of the school and our introductory folder, and that you have completed the relevant paperwork. There is nothing more for me to do but welcome you." He smiled expansively. "As we discussed on the phone, Mr. Ledger, I think there's little point in Philippa and Timothy joining us with only ten days to go to the summer holidays. Far better," he continued, looking from Pip to Tim and back again, "you start fresh in September." He scanned the admission forms on the desk beside him briefly. "Ah!" he exclaimed. "I see you are the new owners of Rawne Barton."

"We moved in yesterday," Mr. Ledger confirmed. "Do you know the place?"

"Indeed, I do," the headmaster replied. "Old Mr. Rawne was most kind to us at the school. He had, I recall, a great interest in the education of young people and invited the year nine history class to visit the house every year. Just prior to his death, he let us conduct an archaeological dig in one of the fields. Nothing terribly ambitious, you understand, but it brought history alive for the students. The resulting coursework folders were exceptional and we had our best-ever history examination results. The science department was also given access to the Garden of Eden for their natural-history project."

"The Garden of Eden?" Pip echoed.

"All fields and many woodlands in the countryside, Philippa, have a government registration number," the headmaster explained, "but many of them also have names that go back hundreds of years. Our school is called Bourne End Comprehensive because it was built on a field of that name in which a bourne, or stream, once ran. At Rawne Barton, the Garden of Eden is a small clump of trees on a hillock down by the river. It never floods, no matter how high the water might come. Miss Hall, our head of biology, says that in the center of the trees there is a circular clearing where some very exotic plants grow."

"When did Mr. Rawne die?" Pip's mother inquired.

"Ten or eleven years ago," Dr. Singall said. "He was in his late eighties, I believe, and had lived alone in the house for about six years, after the death of his wife. At the end, he was only living in a few rooms, with the remainder of the house left unheated and unoccupied. It not surprisingly deteriorated quite rapidly."

"Who inherited it?" asked Mr. Ledger.

"No one exactly," the headmaster responded. "Mr. and Mrs. Rawne had no children, although, during a field trip, I once saw the old man with a young boy. His nephew, I think he told me. He was a pale little chap, didn't look at all well. I would have thought the property might have been left to him or his parents, but it was, in fact, left in trust. The trustees, a law firm in London, only finally wound the trust up two years ago. At least, that is what I've heard. The property was then sold to the developers from whom I assume you purchased it."

Rising from the desk, Dr. Singall opened a glass cabinet on the wall, taking from it a polished wooden box held closed by brass clasps.

"During our dig, we unearthed a lot of quite interesting finds from Rawne's Ground. That's the name of the pasture to the north of the house." He opened the box and started to take items out of it. "A pair of fifteenth-century scissors and a key — rather rusted, I'm afraid." He put them on the blotting pad on his desk. "A broken mortar with its accompanying pestle, a few pieces of what may have been a retort of some sort, some clay pipe stems and this —" he held a small, polished silver disc between his finger and thumb "— which is an English penny dating to the reign of Henry the Fifth. The most intriguing find, however, is this . . ."

From the box, the headmaster gently lifted a tall, thin bottle. It was made of rich blue glass and sealed with a lead plug. When he held it up to the sunlight streaming in through his office window, Pip could see it contained a clear liquid.

"What's in it?" Tim asked.

"We don't know, Timothy," Dr. Singall replied. He tilted the bottle upside down and watched as an air bubble drifted slowly up through the dense, viscous liquid. "As the seal has a curious symbol embossed on it, we assume it might be a medicinal substance of some sort."

He held the bottle at an angle so that they could see the top. Impressed into the dull grey lead was a strange hieroglyph:

"Don't you want to know what the liquid is?" Tim inquired.

"Yes, of course," the headmaster answered, smiling patronizingly at Tim. "Academic curiosity. But it seemed a shame to break the seal to analyze the contents, which are probably nothing more than a common remedy. Castor oil or the like."

"Do you know what the sign means?" Pip asked.

"We do not," the headmaster told her, "but Mr. Carson, our head of geography, informs me it is sometimes used today in meteorology to denote exceptional visibility on a fine day."

He placed everything back in the box carefully and returned it to the cabinet.

"So," the headmaster remarked, addressing Pip and Tim, "when you dig your garden, you'll never know what you might turn up. As we say to the field course students, always watch the blade of your spade! And," he turned to their father, "Mr. Ledger, if you would not be averse to it, I should like very much to revive Mr. Rawne's tradition and bring our history field trip to you next year."

"I'm sure we would be delighted," Pip's father said, rising to his feet.

"Well, I shall see you two in September," the headmaster said to Pip and Tim as they left his office. "Do enjoy the holidays and come back bright-eyed and bushy-tailed."

Pip watched as her parents' car disappeared down the drive, then she returned to carefully unpacking her ornaments and arranging them on her bookcase. It was only when Tim opened the door and walked straight in that her attention was broken.

"Aren't you ever going to remember to knock?" she complained.

"That's what I want to talk to you about," Tim replied.

Pip threw him a look. He reveled in avoiding straight answers. Ask him what time it was and he would reply that supper would be in twenty minutes, the news was on television or, when he last saw a clock about an hour ago, it was coming up to three-thirty.

"Look at this," he continued.

Standing by Pip's door, he started to measure, heel-

to-toe, the distance from the door frame to the wall behind her bed that separated their bedrooms.

"There!" he said. "Five times eighteen centimeters,
the length of my foot. That's about ninety centimeters.
Now come with me."

She followed him into his room, where he did the
same thing, measuring from his door to the separating
wall.

"Four times eighteen — seventy-two centimeters.
All right? So ninety plus seventy-two —"

"Tim," Pip interrupted him. "What are you doing?"

"— makes a hundred and sixty-two centimeters."

"Tim!"

"All will be revealed."

He went into the corridor and started to heel-to-toe
the distance from his door to Pip's.

"Get it?" he asked as he reached her door.

"Get what?" Pip replied, now beginning to lose her
patience.

"Our rooms take up a hundred and sixty-two centimeters, but the distance, door to door, is roughly two
hundred and ninety centimeters. That means the wall's
a hundred and twenty-eight centimeters thick. One
and a quarter meters!"

"So what? It's an old house. They have thick walls."

She turned back into her room, exasperated by Tim's
foray into architectural surveying, and started, once
again, to unpack her ornaments. Tim followed her.

"Did you hear a knocking in the wall last night?" he
asked suddenly.

"Yes," Pip said, somewhat taken aback.

"What do you think it was?"

"The central heating pipes."

"In *summer*?" Tim answered.

"Hot-water pipes, then," Pip retorted. "So what do you suggest?"

"Do you know what a priest's hole is?" Tim asked in his usual infuriating way.

Although she hated to admit it, Pip did not. Once again, Tim, who seemed never to read a book and yet knew an amazing number of obscure facts, had the better of her.

"It was a hiding place for a priest," he went on. "In Tudor times, when Roman Catholicism was banned, rich Catholics hid their ministers to avoid detection and arrest. I think the wall's hollow and the sound traveled upwards —"

"— in a secret chamber," Pip cut in, scornfully. "Well, Tim, you get high marks for imagination."

". . . and if it is hollow," Tim continued, undaunted by his sister's sarcasm, "there must be a way into it somewhere. I've tested the panels in my room. It's not in there. Can I test yours?"

Pip shrugged and lifted a china horse out of the ornament box. Little balls of polystyrene stuck to her arms with static electricity, like fake snowflakes.

"Suit yourself," she said.

Tim knelt by the wall and started tapping his knuckle on the paneling, his ear close to the wood to detect any hollowness. On reaching the panel by Pip's bedside table, he knocked twice. His knock was answered.

"Told you so!" he said, triumphantly. "It echoes."

He knocked again, twice.

Three knocks were returned.

"Some echo!" Tim exclaimed.

"Do it again," Pip said. "Do a pattern." Yet, no sooner had she spoken than she felt suddenly, unaccountably, very afraid.

Tim knocked twice, paused, knocked three times and stopped.

The reply came back: *knock-knock, knock-knock-knock.*

Pip's spine crept: it was as if the blade of a cold knife had been run up her back.

"It must be Dad playing his silly tricks," she muttered.

"They went to the supermarket, remember?" Tim whispered back.

*Knock, knock-knock.*

The first knocks had come from far down in the building. These were nearer.

*Knock. Knock. Knock.*

Each was nearer than the last. It was as if something were rising up through the wall towards them. At any minute, Pip thought, it might burst through the paneling, erupting into her room like the massive claw of a prehistoric monster in a horror film, and reach out to spear her on its slimy talons and drag her to the paneling, where a mouth like an octopus's beak would rip open her chest and suck out her still-breathing lungs.

Tim got quickly to his feet and stepped swiftly away from the wall.

*Knock. Knock.*

Whatever it was, it was now in the paneling right behind Pip's bed. She and her brother exchanged worried glances.

"I'll never sleep here again," she whispered.

"Nor me," Tim murmured. He ran his tongue over his lips. His mouth was dry and his hands clammy with fear. "What do we do?"

"Get out," Pip suggested in an undertone. "Quietly. And when we get to the top of the stairs," she added softly, "run like the devil."

On tiptoe, they started towards the door. The floor-boards creaked out the message of their progress at each step. Pip's heart was racing.

As they went through the door and were about to flee, Tim stopped.

"Listen!"

The knocking had stopped, only to be replaced by an insistent tapping.

"It's not so loud," Pip replied.

"Not that," Tim said. He waited a moment, then added, "That!"

Muffled by the paneling was a voice.

Tim stepped back into the room, Pip grabbing him by the arm.

"What do you think you're doing?" she hissed.

"Listen," Tim said again, but no longer in a whisper.

"Help!" called the muted voice in the wall. "Please help!"

"It's coming from behind your bed," Tim declared. "Give me a hand."

Much against her better judgment, Pip helped her brother pull the bed away from the wall. As she tugged, the thought occurred to her that this might be a trap, that they were being tricked into releasing a demon that had lived for centuries, incarcerated in the walls of the house. Perhaps it was the ghost of a priest long since martyred for his faith, hung, drawn and quartered for conducting Mass. When he appeared, his intestines would be swinging like rotting coils of khaki rope from his belly, one eye dislodged from its socket to roll to and fro across his cheek, suspended by its optic nerve.

The bed reached the center of the room. For a moment, nothing happened. Then, with a barely audible click, a small section of paneling at floor level swung back slowly on heavy, iron hinges. Through the opening appeared the pale face of a boy. He looked as apprehensive as the two faces peering down at him.

"Please, may I beg of you a drink of water?" he asked cautiously.

# Two

# Sebastian's Story

The boy sat on the edge of the bed and sipped a second glass of water, having drained the first in one long gulp.

"I had a great thirst," he explained, breaking the silence, "for it is a long while since last I tasted water. Now that is quenched."

Pip and Tim watched him, bemused. He appeared somehow weak, as if he had just come through a long period of illness, and was dressed in grimy gray flannel shorts, long gray socks, a soiled white shirt and a brown, V-neck pullover. His shoes, which were spotted with mildew and badly needed polishing, were of brown leather with their thin laces tied in a tight bow. He looked, Pip thought, as if he had just stepped out of a film set in the 1950s. All he needed was a little peaked cap with an embroidered school badge on the front.

"You have many questions you would ask me," the boy said, "but first I would know your names and how you come to be here."

Pip told him who they were, how their parents had

bought the house, which had been derelict for some years, and had just moved in.

"What has become of the old man who lived here?" the boy inquired.

"He died," Tim said bluntly. "Was he a relative?"

"Yes," replied the boy, without any sign of emotion. "He was," he paused as if unsure of quite how to describe their relationship, "my uncle."

"But . . . ," Pip replied, somewhat confused and a little shocked that the boy was not upset by the news, ". . . but he died years ago."

"At least ten," Tim added. "You won't remember him. You must have been about two."

"Indeed, I remember him well."

Pip and Tim looked at each other. Neither of them could remember their fifth birthdays clearly, never mind their second.

The boy took another sip of water and said, "There is much I must tell you yet, before I take you into my confidence, I must know if I may trust you."

He closed his eyes for a moment, then, suddenly opening them, stared hard first at Tim, then at Pip. As his gaze fell upon her, Pip felt as if a small electric charge were running through her. Looking down, she noticed the fine hairs on her arms standing up. The sensation lasted only a few seconds.

The boy then smiled and remarked, "We live in a dangerous time and I must be certain of you. Now I know you will be for me." He placed the glass on Pip's bedside table. "Are your parents returned?"

"No," Pip said, wondering how he knew they had gone out, "they won't be back for at least an hour."

"Nevertheless," replied the boy, "please close the door, for what I shall tell you must remain between us. There is much at stake."

As Tim shut the door, the boy left the bed and sat cross-legged on the carpet, signaling for the others to join him. Once they were seated, he leaned forward.

"My name is Sebastian Rawne," he began. "This house was built by my father, and my family has always lived within it. The land was granted to my family in perpetuity by His Majesty, King Henry the Fifth, shortly before his death. My father was in the king's service as . . ."

"Hang on!" Tim interrupted. "You're telling us your father built this place?"

"Yes."

"But, according to the estate agent, it was built in 1422."

"It was begun in 1422," Sebastian corrected him, "yet it was six years in the making."

"Right!" Tim said sardonically.

"Surely you mean your great-great-umpteen-times grandfather built it," Pip suggested.

"No, it was my father, Thomas Rawne."

Tim snorted. "Are you trying to tell us that . . ." he did a quick calculation, ". . . you're coming up for your five hundred and eightieth birthday?"

"I am twelve," Sebastian replied, "yet I was born in 1430. On the first day of July. As it happens," he looked around almost nostalgically, "in this very room. And it was here that, eight days later, my mother died. She gave her life that I might be."

Pip felt a wave of sympathy sweep over her. It was

24

strange to think that anyone could know exactly where they had been born. She and Tim had arrived in one of a dozen identical, anonymous delivery rooms in a huge county hospital. To know also that your mother had died giving birth to you was horrific, and to live in the same house, passing the door to the very room every day, was, she thought, something she could not do.

"This is all rubbish!" Tim retorted.

"Tim!" Pip remonstrated.

Tim looked sheepish and said, "Not about your mother. I mean . . . Well, how can you be nearly six centuries old? It makes no sense."

"I have much to explain," Sebastian admitted, "and you will find what I tell you to be fantastical. Yet I swear to you that all I say shall be the truth, for I live by the truth and will bear no falsehood. I know not where to begin and so will tell you that, although I am but twelve years of age, I have existed for hundreds of years. My age is calculated not by the calendar, but by how long I have been awake."

"Awake!" Tim exclaimed.

"Now that might just make a bit of sense," Pip said, thoughtfully. "You mean you sort of hibernate."

"That is one means by which to explain it," Sebastian replied.

"But animals only hibernate for a few months," Tim reasoned. "Like a tortoise or a bear, going through the winter. They don't turn off for *years*."

"Lungfish do," Pip said. "I saw a documentary on the Discovery Channel. They can lie dormant in dried mud for years."

"Does he look like a fish to you?" Tim rejoined.

"My father," Sebastian said quietly, "discovered a potion, which he called *aqua soporiferum*, the water that induces sleep. By means of this, one can slow the functions of the body. When I am not awake, my heart beats but six times an hour and I breathe but once in twenty minutes, and then only shallowly. My body cools and, as it does so, my brain ceases to function in the ordinary fashion."

"But how do you wake up?" Pip wanted to know. "What makes you?"

"That I shall tell you soon," Sebastian said. "But now, I must request of you some food, for I have a terrible hunger now that my thirst is slaked."

Tim checked that they were alone in the house, and they went downstairs to the kitchen, where Pip set about preparing a meal for Sebastian. There wasn't much in the cupboards except cans and jars brought from the previous house, but she found a beef and ale pie in a flat, circular tin and heated it up in the oven. While that was cooking she gave him a bowl of cream of tomato soup and slices of bread and butter. Whatever was placed before him, Sebastian ate with gusto, wolfing it down as if he were starving. He also drank a liter of milk and a Pepsi, which, he remarked, tasted most curious.

"We've got to get you some different clothes," Tim commented as Sebastian started on a packet of chocolate digestive biscuits. "Yours look as if they're about to fall apart."

"Would you like to wash while we find you something to wear?" Pip asked.

"I should very much like to bathe," Sebastian said, "for my flesh is still cold. As for my clothes, they are over sixty years old. They were, briefly, my school uniform. Just for the summer term of 1939. A truancy officer visited the house and my uncle and aunt had to send me to school to comply with his demands. On the third of September, war was declared with Nazi Germany. There was much confusion thereafter that autumn, so I did not return."

"What about when you were . . ." Tim was not sure how to phrase it, ". . . when you were a little boy? Didn't you go to school then?"

"Indeed not. There were the universities at Oxford and Cambridge, but schools were very few. The monasteries educated young boys, but, mostly, only if they were to enter the service of Our Lord. The King's College of Our Lady at Eton beside Windsor was not founded until the year I was — or, rather, I would have been — ten. And the Church was not to be my destiny."

"So who taught you?" Tim asked.

"My father taught me. I was to follow his profession. It was the way then."

With the dirty plates in the dishwasher, they took Sebastian upstairs and ran a hot bath for him. While he lay in the steaming water, Tim went into his room, where, after rummaging about in his chest of drawers, he produced a pair of jeans, a T-shirt and sweatshirt, as well as a pair of underpants and socks. In place of Sebastian's shoes, he found a pair of old sneakers. Hoping the clothes would fit, he pushed them around the bathroom door.

27

"Now you look the man!" Tim said, as the new Sebastian entered Pip's room. "I'm sorry if the shoes whiff a bit."

Sebastian studied himself in Pip's full-length mirror, evidently pleased by what he had been given.

"You said you were to follow in your father's footsteps. Is that right?" Pip asked.

"In a manner of speaking, yes."

"What did your father do?" Tim inquired.

Sebastian turned from the mirror to face them both. "My father," he said, "was the court alchemist to King Henry the Fifth and King Henry the Sixth."

"An alchemist . . . ." Pip began.

From outside came the sound of a car door slamming shut.

Tim ran to the window and hissed, "Mum and Dad are back."

Sebastian went quickly to the open panel in the wall and eased himself through it.

"I shall return," he said, his face framed by the sides of the secret door. "Be ready after midnight. I have much yet to tell and show you."

Pip and Tim slid the bed towards the window so as not to obstruct the hidden entrance, then went downstairs, ready to explain away the empty tins in the bin and the dirty plates in the dishwasher.

After tea, Pip and Tim walked down to the river. Beneath the overhang of a weeping willow stood an old oak bench. It had clearly not been used in a long while, for the slats of the seat were mottled with lichen and the back was stained with dried squirts of bird droppings. Half submerged in the water was a rowing boat, its rotting mooring rope still tied to a root of the willow. The evening sun shone through the trees across the water meadows on the far bank. In a reedy creek over the river, an unseen moorhen was calling. Beyond it, a heron stalked meticulously through the long buttercup- and daisy-filled grass, watching for frogs, newts or eels.

Side by side, they sat on the bench. It was some minutes before Tim finally spoke.

"Do you actually think he's for real?"

Pip considered all that had happened and said, "What other explanation can there be?"

"He can be lying through his teeth," Tim remarked. "I mean, it's ridiculous! He says he's twelve going on six hundred. The oldest person ever to have lived was only a hundred and twenty-two. I looked it up on the Internet. As for hibernation: a few months, maybe, but years at a stretch?"

"I've been thinking about that," Pip replied. "What about a coma? People can be in a coma for years."

"And then they die," Tim said. "Comas are caused by brain damage."

"Sometimes they come out of it. No one knows why. What if," Pip speculated, "you could control a coma? Like, with meditation? So it's not a coma but a sort of a trance. And there's something else. When some young children fall through the ice on freezing ponds, it's sometimes up to thirty minutes before the rescuers get them out. You'd think they'd drown, but they don't. With the sudden shock of hitting the icy water, they stop breathing and their brains close down. He told us his body went cold. What's more, he said his father had found out how to do it."

"All right," Tim allowed. "But what about his father being an alchemist? You know what alchemists did? Or *said* they did, more like." He did not wait for his sister's response. "They turned iron into gold. Like, yes?" He gave a short, sarcastic laugh. "And we're meant to believe he was an expert in human medicine too? C'mon, sis, wake up and smell the toast burning."

"But," Pip persisted, "if he was lying, then what's the truth? He came out of a secret passage in an old house, dressed in clothes Grandad would have worn as a schoolboy. And the way he talks. It's not exactly Bart Simpson, is it?"

Tim picked up a twig and tossed it into the river. The moorhen, alarmed by the splash, took to the wing, its feet stepping across the surface as if it were walking upon the water.

"Dungeons and Dragons," he replied, watching as the moorhen veered clumsily and vanished into a bed of bulrushes. "He could have picked up that kind of thing watching Robin Hood movies."

"Maybe . . ." Pip mused.

They stood up and set off along the riverbank. The grounds of Rawne Barton included a quarter of a mile of river frontage and, as they walked in silence, Tim watched out for likely pools and eddies where trout might linger and he might fly-fish for them.

"In some ways, he's scary," Pip went on. "He seems so . . . so self-contained. And what was all that about living in a dangerous time and having to be certain of us? When he stared at us, I went all goose pimply."

"Look, when a teacher stands in front of the class, glares at you and says, 'Right, who shoved a pencil up the classroom hamster's bottom? Own up or else,' you feel like that, don't you? Even though you didn't do it, and you know you didn't do it, you still feel squirmy. It's the same thing."

"Yes," Pip replied. "And yet . . ."

It was not until they reached the hedge marking the boundary with the neighboring farm fields, and turned to walk back across the pasture to the house, that they spoke again.

"The thing is," Tim said, "whatever the facts are, do we trust him?"

"He did say he'd tell the truth," Pip reminded her brother. "Besides, what have we got to lose? We don't know anyone around here and we probably won't meet anyone before the term starts. That's the whole summer away."

In the glow of the late sun, the brickwork of the house seemed to radiate a deep, abiding warmth, the sunlight on the windows looking as if the building were alight with a mysterious fire. The shadows of the ancient trees were long upon the grass.

As they drew near to the house, Tim said, "Anyway, I bet he turns out to be just a local lamebrain. Still," he finished, "you're right. We might as well hang out with him. There's no one else."

# Three

# Sub Terra

Pip lay fully dressed on her bed, listening. Not for the first time, she checked her alarm clock. The digital numbers flickered — *12:14.*

There was a quiet, metallic rattle. Pip watched the latch on her bedroom door slowly lift and click. Gradually, bit by bit, the door opened and a dark figure entered. The door closed quietly.

"Has he turned up?" the figure whispered, barely audible.

"No. Not yet."

Tim switched on his Mini Maglite, running the narrow beam quickly over the wall panel. Pip could see he was also fully dressed, in jeans and a dark sweatshirt.

"Snug under a duvet somewhere," Tim muttered ruefully.

Yet no sooner had he spoken than there came slight scuffling sounds from within the wall. The panel opened to show Sebastian's face hanging as if suspended in the darkness.

"Hello," he murmured. "I regret my tardiness.

Sometimes when I awake it takes me a few days to adjust."

"A bit like being jet-lagged," Pip suggested.

"Like he would know?" said Tim. "They had intercontinental jet travel in the 1400s?"

Sebastian stepped out into the room. He was wearing the clothes Tim had found for him but, over the T-shirt, he had added a sort of coarse, woolen, long-sleeved pullover with a square-cut neck. It hung loosely upon him as if it were several sizes too big. Upon the front was sewn, in silver thread, a design like a jag of lightning.

"Cool jersey," Tim remarked.

"It is a tabard," Sebastian explained. "Men wore it to cover their armor." He adjusted it over his shoulders. "I wish now to take you to my chamber," he added. "It is not far." Reaching out, he touched both of them lightly on the arm. "Will you follow me?" he said softly. "Take care, for the steps are much worn in the center."

With that, he stepped back towards the wall and seemed to disappear without even having to bend down.

Pip went first, sitting on the floor and lowering herself feet first through the panel, to discover a tightly spiraled staircase beyond it. With her hands pressed to the wall on either side, she started to descend. The glimmer of Tim's flashlight behind her was the only source of light.

Reaching the bottom of the steps, some of which were — as Sebastian had warned — well worn, Pip was confronted by a low and narrow stone passageway. The roof was arched and the floor set with flagstones. Sebastian was waiting there.

"We have but a short distance remaining," he said, adding, "and Tim, will you please extinguish your source of light?"

"But it's as black as a badger's hole down here," Tim replied.

"You will not require illumination," Sebastian explained. "The way will show itself unto you."

As Pip started off down the passage, Tim switched off his flashlight and immediately felt disoriented. It was as if he were suddenly suspended in a black liquid. He reached out to feel the wall, partly to comfort himself and partly to keep his balance. The stones were cool and surprisingly dry.

"Touch not the wall," Sebastian said.

His voice seemed far off. Tim reckoned he had already gone some way down the passage, although there had been no sound of his retreating footsteps.

"You there, Pip?" Tim asked.

"Over here," she replied, yet her voice also seemed distant.

Without being exactly sure that he was heading in the right direction, Tim took a tentative step forward. When he did not bang his head against the wall, he took another, then another, then another. It seemed as if he were not so much walking as the floor of the passageway was shifting under him, like a slow-moving treadmill in a gym.

Suddenly, the passage ended in an open door made of heavy planks of dark wood joined together with iron

34

bolts. Although Tim was sure she had been some way ahead of him in the passage, Pip was only just passing through the door as he arrived, a few steps away.

Sebastian was waiting for them in a large, vaulted chamber lit by four candles set in bronze wall mountings. It was about ten meters square and four high. At the center of the arched ceiling the ribs of the vaulting met in a large stone boss into which was mounted an iron hook. From this hung an iron gantry and a series of chains and pulleys. In the middle of the room stood a vast oak table upon which was arranged a collection of glass retorts and copper distillation condensers, a tripod, ceramic dishes, iron or pewter bowls, a mortar made of alabaster, racks of bottles and a pile of leather-bound volumes.

A library of other books lined shelves on one wall, stretching from floor to ceiling, the top levels reached by a set of sliding library steps fixed to brass runners on the penultimate shelf. In an alcove opposite the door was a stone platform with several thickly fleeced sheepskins spread upon it. Animal hides covered the floor like carpets. The only other furniture consisted of several high stools by the table, some lower stools and two massive oak chests with iron padlocks from which protruded enormous keys. The whole place smelled of dust, stone and something sweet, like dried orange peel.

"This is my domain," Sebastian announced. "It is humble, yet it serves my purpose well, for I have no need of greater comforts."

"Where exactly are we?" Pip asked, as she and Tim gazed around themselves in amazement.

Sebastian avoided the question. "Please," he indicated two of the low stools, "be seated, for we must talk."

As Pip and Tim lowered themselves onto the stools, Sebastian went to the table and, taking a bottle from a rack, pulled the cork.

"I wish to show you something," he said. "You need not be afraid, but it will be strange." He held the bottle out. "Close your eyes and, when I request it, inhale through your nose. Not too deeply. No more than you would to smell a delicately scented flower."

Pip closed her eyes. Tim followed her example, although with some hesitation. Sebastian held the bottle under their nostrils for a few moments, then, corking it again, said, "Open your eyes."

"Wow!" Tim exclaimed, his hands gripping the seat of his stool as if he were afraid it might suddenly throw him off.

The entire room seemed vast, like a cathedral nave. The walls were deep purple and the flagstones seemed to be shifting as if turning to liquid.

"What do you hear, Pip?" Sebastian asked.

"Weird music," Pip replied. "It sounds like . . ." she sought for the right description ". . . like the song of whales."

"Close your eyes once more and take a deep breath," Sebastian ordered.

They did as they were told and, when they opened their eyes again, the chamber was as it had been.

"How did you . . . ." Tim began.

"With ease," Sebastian said, grinning. "And, in time, you shall understand." He perched himself upon

36

one of the tall stools and looked down at them. "First, I must ask you if you know of alchemy."

"It's a sort of magic, isn't it?" Tim ventured. "People tried to turn iron into gold with it."

"It is what today you would call science," Sebastian explained. "It has many aims, of which the transmutation of base metal into gold was but one. In the main, the alchemist aspired first to transform common and useless substances into rare, useful matter; second, to prolong life indefinitely and cure disease and aging; third, to produce life from nonliving matter, ultimately to create a homunculus."

"A what?" Pip asked.

"A homunculus is an artificial human being, born not of woman."

"Like an android?"

"Somewhat," Sebastian replied.

"This is all crapola!" Tim retorted. "Making gold out of scrap iron and men out of mud."

"Perhaps not," Sebastian said. "Consider what science has already achieved. Cannot gold be fashioned in a thermonuclear reactor? Or diamonds created from carbon under intense pressure and heat? Have not rare elements — the actinides — been produced by men? Nobelium, lawrencium with a half-life of but thirteen seconds, mendelevium, made by bombarding einsteinium with alpha particles in a particle accelerator . . ."

As he spoke, Pip and Tim just looked at him. Pip wondered how on Earth he knew so much, especially when he had spent all but twelve years or so of the last six centuries asleep and had presumably only recently woken up. It was then she remembered the headmaster

37

mentioning the old man's nephew. He must have seen Sebastian. As for Tim, he was curious about what *half-life* meant and what actinides were, and resolved to look them up on the Web at the first opportunity.

"It may yet be impossible to prolong life indefinitely, but are there not medicines to conquer illness?" Sebastian continued. "Is not the Human Genome Project and the study of DNA providing cures for genetic diseases? And is it not possible to implant into one man the heart of another, that he might live longer?"

"Yes," Pip admitted.

Tim was not going to be so easily swayed.

"So! They can transplant hearts and livers and kidneys," he said, "but making a man . . ."

"Why not?" Sebastian replied. "Are there not fertility methods to create children within the womb? Have not human embryos been formed within test tubes? Do you not know of cloning? Has not a sheep been cloned? If a man can produce a sheep by artificial means, why not a homunculus?"

Sebastian turned to the table and opened one of the leather-bound tomes, fingering carefully through the pages.

"Lamebrain?" Pip whispered to her brother.

Tim looked nonplussed.

"In the sixteenth century," Sebastian began, "the alchemist, Paracelsus, stated that he produced a golem, one foot high."

"A golem?" Pip asked.

"It is the ancient Hebrew word for a homunculus," Sebastian replied, "for such creatures have long been thought to exist, from well before the time of Christ,

Our Lord. Paracelsus, however, could not control it and it fled from him." He held the book out. "You may read of it here."

Pip and Tim leaned forward. The text on the page used the English alphabet, but they could only recognize a few of the words. The typeface of the printing was ornate, with complicated illuminated capital letters at the start of every paragraph.

"Does it say how he made this creature?" Tim inquired.

"Paracelsus writes that he placed bones, skin and hair from a human in the ground beneath a midden of horse manure. After forty days, an embryo formed . . ."

"And you believe that!" Tim exclaimed.

"Once, yes, I did," Sebastian admitted, matter-of-factly. "Yet now I am wiser."

He closed the book and put it back on the table.

"Alchemy's bunk!" Tim declared.

Sebastian smiled and asked, "Tim, what time is it?"

Tim looked at his watch.

"Twenty-five to one," he answered.

Sebastian picked up a small glass rod from the table and struck it gently against the wood. It vibrated like a tuning fork. When the tiny hum had almost died away, he got down from his high stool and, after briefly pressing the base of the rod against his own wrist, touched it against Tim's. A tiny throbbing pulse momentarily tickled his skin.

"Now regard your timepiece, Tim," Sebastian ordered.

Tim studied his digital watch. There seemed nothing unusual about it. The seconds were still ticking by, yet, as they reached *oo*, the minute number did not change.

"You see," Sebastian exclaimed, "there are things an alchemist may do that even modern science has yet to achieve."

"Those vibrations have upset the chip in my Seiko," Tim said, somewhat peeved. He had been given the watch only the previous Christmas, and he tapped the glass in the hope that he might jar it into working properly.

"On the contrary," Sebastian replied, "the electronic components of your timepiece are unaffected. And your striking it will not affect it, for it has no moving parts. Look instead at your sister."

Tim turned. Pip was sitting beside him just as she had been, but her face was set in a stare at the far wall. She did not seem to be breathing.

"What've you done to her?" Tim said, his voice filled with worry for his sister, his anger rising sharply.

"Do not be concerned," Sebastian continued. "Pip is well but she is in another time. You see, Tim, I have made time pause for you and me."

"That's not possible . . . ." Tim began, but Sebastian held his hand up to silence him.

"Consider time," he said, "to be like a book." He picked a thin volume up off the table, the ancient leather binding scarred and worn. "Think of this book as being time. It is all happening at once." He opened a page halfway through. "It is as if we are on this page, yet Pip," he thumbed over a leaf, "is here. She is waiting for us to catch her up."

"But for her it's going on?" Tim asked.

"Yes. Only in relation to you and me, time is frozen for her. On this other page, you and Pip and I are talking. I am telling you that you must go now and, in a few moments, I shall say that I shall see you again on the morrow."

"So let me get my head around this," Tim said, still somewhat confused. "According to your theory, at this moment, somewhere else in time — on another page — the Duke of Wellington is winning the battle of Waterloo, Henry Ford is making his first car and the Beatles are topping the charts?"

"Precisely!" Sebastian exclaimed. "Yet this is not theory. Do you know the feeling of *déjà vu*?"

"That's when you do something, or experience something, for the first time, but feel that you've done it before," Tim said.

"You are correct. It occurs when, for a fleeting moment, it is as if you accidentally have a brief glimpse of being on another page within the book that is time."

Tim thought for a moment before he asked, "Is doing this time-stopping trick, plus using your father's method of slowing down your bodily functions, how you hibernate?"

Sebastian did not answer the question directly, but smiled. "It is not a trick, Tim. And I show you this as a lesson you must heed. Do not," he advised, his voice quiet and earnest, "refuse that which you do not understand. Question it, yes — but never dismiss it until you know the truth of it."

Picking up the glass rod, Sebastian held it at its ends.

"Shall we rejoin Pip?" he suggested, and, with a sharp crack, snapped the rod in two and dropped the pieces on the table.

Tim's body shook briefly, as if he were sitting in a car going over a bad pothole. To his surprise, he found himself no longer sitting on the low stool, but on his feet. Pip was standing beside him. Glancing at his watch, he noticed it read *12:38.*

"Now, I have tasks to which I must attend," Sebastian said. "There is much preparation to be done. I shall come again in the forenoon, when I must explain to you why I am awakened."

Showing Pip and Tim to the door through which they had entered, Sebastian told them, as before, just to keep walking and not to touch the walls. Before they had taken a step, the door closed solidly behind them and they were left in pitch darkness.

"Charming!" Tim exclaimed softly.

No sooner had he spoken than he suddenly felt very afraid. The space between his shoulder blades itched as if someone — or something — were watching him. He involuntarily turned his head, but there was nothing behind him, only blackness. Fumbling in his pocket, he found his Maglite and twisted the end to switch it on. Nothing happened. The batteries were new. He banged it on the palm of his hand. It still refused to come on.

"Pip . . . ." he said, anxiously.

There was no reply.

"Pip!" he hissed loudly.

Still, there was only silence.

Now afraid, Tim started walking briskly, almost

breaking into a jog. At any moment, he hoped to catch up with his sister. Gradually, he realized that the floor of the passageway had become steps, each positioned to measure his stride. He slowed and continued to climb, the steps spiraling round. In less than a minute, he found himself in Pip's room, although he did not remember having to crawl through the opening in the panel to get there.

Pip was woken at nine o'clock by someone shaking her shoulder firmly.

"Come along, slug-a-bed!"

She opened her eyes. Her mother was leaning over her.

"This isn't like you, Pip! You're usually up with the lark. At least," she added, "in summer."

As her mother opened the curtains, letting the bright, clear morning sunlight shine in, Pip sat up, rubbed her eyes and ran her fingers through her sleep-tousled hair.

"Is Tim up?" she asked.

"I've just been in to see him. And there's a boy called Sebastian downstairs come to visit you," she added. "I didn't know you'd made any friends around here. That was quick!"

Gathering her wits quickly about her, Pip said, "We only met him yesterday. He's . . . ." she grasped for something to say that was not a lie, without being the entire truth, ". . . the son of someone who used to live here."

"Fancy that!" her mother responded.

43

It took Pip less than ninety seconds to dress. Hurrying out of her bedroom, she met Tim at the top of the staircase.

"It's all true," he said.

"What is?"

"*Actinides, mendelevium, half-life.* I logged on last night. A half-life is the length of time it takes half the nuclei of a radioactive element to decay. He knows all about nuclear physics. And the Human Genome Project — that's a worldwide study of the genetics of the entire human race."

"I don't see how . . . ." Pip began.

"And that's not all. Last night, do you remember him tapping a glass rod on the table?"

"Yes."

"What happened next?"

Pip thought for a moment and said, "He touched your wrist with it, then he snapped it in two."

"And what happened between those two actions?"

"What do you mean?" Pip asked. "Nothing."

"Yes, it did," Tim said. "He took me off to another page in time."

"A what?"

He briefly explained Sebastian's theory to Pip.

"You mean he can travel through time?" she asked at length. "That's a question scientists have pondered over for centuries."

"Well," Tim said, "it seems someone's found the answer."

They exchanged glances and descended the stairs.

"Your friend tells me he hasn't had breakfast yet," their mother announced as Pip and Tim entered the kitchen to find Sebastian standing by the back door, "so you can all have something together."

She poured out three glasses of orange juice and placed packets of cereal on the table with a jug of milk. They helped themselves to bowls of cornflakes, sitting side by side at the table.

"I understand from Pip that you used to live here, Sebastian?"

"Yes, but when I was younger," Sebastian admitted between mouthfuls of cereal.

"Was Mr. Rawne your father?" she asked, with apparent innocence.

"He was."

Pip looked at Tim. This was their mother's way: pose seemingly innocuous questions until she could entrap you, then move in for the kill.

"I have heard he was in his eighties," Mrs. Ledger said. "Surely he wasn't your father!"

"No," Sebastian answered. "He who lived here was my uncle. My father left the house long before and my uncle lived here thereafter with my aunt. But she died a long time ago."

"Your uncle?" she replied, clearly doubting the statement. "Surely not your father's brother?"

Sebastian shook his head and said, "He was actually a distant relative of my father's. I only called him uncle when I was with him."

"And tell me, where do your parents live now?"

Sebastian, not in the least fazed by this inquisition, replied, "My mother has passed on."

"Oh! I am so dreadfully sorry," Mrs. Ledger said, taken aback by Sebastian's forthrightness.

45

She was about to go on with her probing when she was interrupted by a buzzing sound coming from the alarm-system panel on the wall by the fridge.

"That's the carpet fitters," Mrs. Ledger said. "Now you three eat up and run along. Don't get underfoot. I'll be busy all morning."

"That was close!" Tim whispered, as his mother left the room. "She was out to trip you up."

"I am aware of this," Sebastian remarked. "It is a mother's way with strangers."

When their breakfast was over, they left the house, Sebastian suggesting that they walk down towards the river. It was a perfect summer's day, the sky blue and dotted with fair-weather clouds, the shade of the trees deep and close. Where the grass was long, tiny aquamarine butterflies no bigger than a fingernail flitted between the stems. Here and there, unseen grasshoppers sawed and chirruped.

Reaching the first of the massive oaks, Sebastian paused and said quietly, "This tree was planted by my father. In 1430, the day after my birth."

"Do you remember your father?" Pip asked.

"Indeed," Sebastian replied, "I was ten years of age when I saw him die."

"What!" Tim exclaimed. "What do you mean?"

"It was here," Sebastian said, halting halfway between the oak and a towering beech tree. "On this spot. I will show you."

He bent to the ground where a mole had turned over the earth, and started to dig with his fingers. After excavating a hole only a few centimeters deep, he

46

picked up a handful of soil. It was moist and dark gray, filled with little chips of what looked like black gravel.

"This is charcoal," he explained. "This field is wet because of the river and so the charcoal has been preserved." He brushed the earth from his fingers. "It was here, in the month of May in the year of Our Lord 1440, that my father was burned at the stake, accused of witchcraft."

"That's awful," Pip said, feeling the tears well up in her eyes, fighting them back and swallowing the lump forming in her throat.

"My father had powerful enemies," Sebastian continued calmly. "They did not want him to use his skills on behalf of the king, whom they feared. They came one night and arrested him. There was a trial held, in the chamber that you now call your living room. My father, who was seated before the fireplace, was resigned to his fate. He knew that they would find him guilty."

"Wasn't there anyone to speak up for him? A friend or a lawyer or something?" Tim said.

Sebastian smiled faintly. "That was not the way it was," he replied. "Once my father was arrested, they sought to keep away. They, too, were afraid."

"Were you present at the trial?" Pip asked tentatively, wiping a finger across her cheek to smooth away the first tear to escape.

"I was, for my father's accusers wanted me to see the wages of his sins. They knew that he would have been instructing me in his knowledge and they wished to discourage me from furthering his researches." He patted down the earth of the molehill with his foot and

47

started to walk slowly on towards the river. "The trial was a short proceeding, lasting but a day. When it was over, and the sentence pronounced, my father was taken in chains and locked into your room, Tim. It was there I was brought to him, to make my farewells."

He paused as if recalling the event. At that moment, it occurred to Tim that, so far as Sebastian's waking time was concerned, all this had happened only two years before. The pain, he thought, must still be there.

"My father had known they would come for him eventually," Sebastian continued. "He had told me often before that he was playing a dangerous game, one that he must win." Reaching out, he touched Pip's hand. "There is no need to cry," he comforted her. "It was a long time ago and I do not grieve."

They reached the river, where Sebastian sat down on the bank beside a clump of willow. The warm breeze blowing along the water whispered gently in the upright withy stems, tickling the long, thin leaves. Upstream, a mute swan was riding the current, accompanied by four gray, fluff-feathered cygnets.

"Have you lived here . . . ." Tim began — he wanted to say, all your life — ". . . since you were born?"

"Yes," Sebastian answered, "and there is good reason, for here is much wickedness which must be fought."

"Wickedness?" Tim said.

Pip was alarmed and asked hesitantly, "You mean — in our house?"

"No, but hereabouts. In the countryside." Sebastian leaned back on his elbows while Pip and Tim squatted on the riverbank. "The night before they came for my father," he went on, "he took me aside into his chamber, the one that you have visited. Here, he charged me with continuing his mission. But to understand this, you must know something of history."

"Not my favorite subject," Tim announced.

Sebastian looked around, as if to ensure they were not being overheard, then spoke in a subdued voice.

"King Henry the Fifth was a great monarch, the most powerful ruler in Europe. He won the famous battle against the French at Agincourt and captured Normandy. Then he made peace with the King of France and married his daughter. Soon, they had a son, named after his father; yet he was but an infant of nine months when his father died and he was proclaimed King Henry the Sixth. Immediately, Humphrey, Duke of Gloucester, claimed to be regent, ruling in the infant's stead. He was a man who much wanted power. However, the council of those in control did not wish this and appointed Gloucester's older brother, John, Duke of Bedford, as regent."

"So the second king your father served was only a baby," Pip said.

"Yes," Sebastian replied, "yet he was still the rightful monarch and it was to him and his throne my father owed his allegiance."

"And," Tim said, "because your father was a king's man, he got caught up in the struggle between these two brothers. Right?"

"You are almost correct," Sebastian replied. "The struggle was not so much between Gloucester and Bedford as between Gloucester and his uncle, Henry Beaufort, who was the wealthiest man in England, a power behind many thrones and my father's friend and patron.

He was Chancellor of England, a cardinal of the Pope in Rome and Bishop of Winchester. He was also interested in alchemy."

"Hang on!" Tim interjected. "He was a cardinal and a bishop but he believed in alchemy?"

"Pope Leo III gave the emperor, Charlemagne, a book on alchemy called the *Enchiridion*," Sebastian said, "and Pope Sylvester II is said to have practiced magic. Yet this is by the way . . ." He paused as if to gather his interrupted chain of thought. "Gloucester knew he was no match for Henry Beaufort and so he traveled to France, where he took into his commission a French alchemist by the name of Pierre de Loudéac. They struck an alliance. If de Loudéac would help Gloucester gain power, he, in turn, would withdraw the British from Normandy. Henry Beaufort came to hear of this and entreated my father to use his knowledge to defeat that of de Loudéac."

"What was de Loudéac's plan?" Pip asked.

"It was simple," Sebastian answered. "He was going to make a homunculus to replace the infant king."

While Sebastian had been talking, the swan had moved slowly downstream and was now drifting towards the reeds on the opposite bank, her cygnets keeping close. Sebastian watched them for a moment, then stood up, brushing dry leaves and dirt from his jeans. He set off along the riverbank. Pip and Tim followed him.

"Did he succeed?" Tim wanted to know.

"No. He failed."

"What has all this got to do with you?" Pip asked. "It all happened centuries ago."

Sebastian made no response until he was well away from the willows.

"That is so," he eventually replied, casting a sideways look at the swan, which was continuing downstream, its wings set like parallel sails, "yet, after the attempt to re-place the infant king had failed, de Loudéac persevered with his quest to make a homunculus."

"So what . . . ?" Tim began.

"It is a vital matter," Sebastian interrupted him. "A homunculus is more than just an artificial creature. It is a living human, yet one that has no soul." He fell silent, to give this fact time to sink in.

"What you're saying," Pip said, after a pause, "is that this . . . *thing* isn't just a created man, but one that, if it has no soul, has no mind of its own."

"Exactly so!" Sebastian came back. "This creature, without its own free will, may be commanded by its maker."

"I don't see the problem," Tim declared. "It might be unnatural, but . . ."

Sebastian sighed. "You see nothing wrong in an evil man being able to create a creature — or many crea-tures — that will do his every bidding?"

"Wow!" Tim held his hands up. "This is way too sci-fi! Any minute now," he added skeptically, "we'll have some Hollywood hulk charging over the hill, toting a laser gun, with half his computer-generated skull split open to show the circuit boards inside, and liquidizing anyone that gets in his way."

"You may be flippant, Tim," Sebastian said curtly, his voice growing agitated, "but what I tell you is fact.

De Loudéac has, through the centuries, not given up on his quest — and he continues to this very day."

"C'mon!" Tim said. "You've got to admit it's a bit off the wall. Like, what's he going to do with this flesh-and-blood robot? As he failed to get power over Henry the Sixth, what's next? Take over the royal family? Turn them into zombies? Clone them? Rule England? Rule the world?"

"These may well be his intentions, for has he not already sought to overthrow the established throne of England?" Sebastian rejoined, continuing, "Of this I can be sure. Whatever his plans, he seeks to do terrible wrong in the world by his creation and, should he achieve his end, it will mean much danger. If he were to fashion a homunculus, there would be abroad in the land a creature of infinite malevolence, a fearful beast spawned of great iniquity, capable of bringing such wickedness as you would never have known, nor could imagine. Therefore, it is imperative," he went on, his voice calming, "that I succeed in foiling de Loudéac's plan, prevent him from reaching his objective. Should I fail, it will be the beginning of chaos and an age of evil will commence that may destroy all we know as good."

"Don't you think that's just a teensy bit OTT?" Tim replied. "I mean, this is the stuff of Superman."

"OTT?" Sebastian asked.

"Over the top," Tim explained. "Too much. Way out. Implausible. Like, *really* unlikely."

"No," Sebastian answered tersely. "This is not. It is, I assure you, plausible."

"Like, yes . . . ." Tim said, yet, as he looked at Sebastian, he saw he was in deadly earnest, his face set.

Pip, who had been thinking while the others argued, asked, "What do you mean, 'continues to this very day'?" No sooner had she spoken than she wondered if she wanted to hear the answer.

"I mean," Sebastian said, "that de Loudéac is here, now, pursuing this end."

Tim thought for a moment and said, "But how can he be here?"

"He can," Sebastian replied, "because, when my father was arrested and tried, de Loudéac was present. It was he who was my father's accuser. And he acquired a bottle of *aqua soporiferum*."

"So you have seen him!" Pip exclaimed.

"Yes," Sebastian confirmed, "I have seen him many times."

"What does he look like?" she asked.

"If this de Loudéac has a bottle of your father's gloop," Tim mused aloud, "he must be able to hibernate like you."

"Indeed, he can," Sebastian said. Then, looking from Pip to her brother and back again, his eyes seeking out theirs, he went on, "Understand this, you live in a time of great peril, for de Loudéac has returned. Whenever he is awake, I am awake, for my father trained me thus. This is my mission, my task. I must combat de Loudéac and stop him in his endeavors. To do this, I require your assistance."

He looked down the river, shading the sunlight from his face with his hand.

"Wherever I am," Sebastian added, "he will be trying to overhear what I say, studying my actions, seeking a way to defeat me. And if you are my accomplices, he will seek to undo you as well. Of this you must be aware. I do not demand your help, I only request it for I fear I am not able to defeat him alone."

"Say no more!" Tim replied, the excitement rising in him. "We're on your train, my man!"

Sensing Tim's levity, Sebastian warned, "This is not a game we play, Tim. It is a deadly enterprise upon which we are engaged. Much lies at stake, for, if de Loudéac succeeds, there will be on Earth a man not born of woman who will answer only to the darkness. And to his creator."

"We're still with you," Pip said, "but one thing I don't understand. Why, when he could go anywhere in the world, does he return here?"

"Because here," Sebastian explained, "is where the powers of good and the powers of evil come together. You know of Stonehenge?"

"Yes," Pip replied.

"It is a place where natural power is centered. The ancient people knew this and built there to attempt to harness it. De Loudéac comes here for the same purpose." Looking beyond Pip and Tim, he lowered his voice to little more than a whisper. "You asked what de Loudéac looked like. He appears as he wishes you to see him." Sebastian raised his hand and pointed beyond the willows. "Behold him now."

Pip and Tim spun round. In the middle of the river, six meters away from where they had been talking, was another swan.

It was black.

No sooner had they seen the swan than it took flight. They watched as its wings beat the air, the flight

54

feathers whistling as it gained height, banked and disappeared over the water meadows across the river. When it was gone, Sebastian left Pip and Tim, saying that he would meet them in the afternoon at the rear of the coach house.

The black swan had unnerved Pip and, although Tim discovered from the Internet that there were such things as black swans, that they were indigenous to Australia and that there were a small number in Britain, living exclusively on the lakes in the royal parks of London, her mind was not put at rest.

"I expect they lose one or two every year," Tim said, by way of explanation. "They fly away to look for a mate or go on their holidays or something."

"London's over a hundred miles away," Pip said.

"So what?" Tim was determined to justify the black swan and reduce his sister's fears. "Bewick's swans migrate here from Arctic Siberia and whooper swans from Greenland. A quick jaunt down the motorway would be nothing."

Yet, despite his reasoning, Tim could not help wondering if the swan really had been de Loudéac. It was fast becoming plain to him, as it was to Pip, that nothing could necessarily be taken at face value any longer.

Shortly after two o'clock, Pip and Tim approached the coach house. It was about fifty meters from the main house, across what had once been a cobbled courtyard but was now a graveled turning circle with an oval of lawn in the center, ringed by beds of roses. A spur of raked gravel led off to the former stables, now converted into a two-car garage and a garden store, but only a dirt path went to the coach house.

"What did the estate agent say? 'In need of reno-vation'?" Tim remarked as he surveyed the tenacious ivy- and moss-covered stone walls, broken window frames and double oak doors clearly half off their hinges. "In need of bulldozing and starting again, more like."

They turned the corner of the building, avoiding a dense patch of nettles and deadly nightshade, one or two of its little faint violet flowers drooping from the top of the tall stem. Lower down were two ripe berries, as black and as shiny as onyx.

The land beyond the coach house was wilder than the meadows near the river and more undulating. The grass was long and in dire need of cutting for hay. The trees seemed more unkempt and the distant overgrown hedgerow had clearly not been trimmed for a long time and should have been laid years before.

Sebastian was waiting for them, standing in the long grass some way behind the coach house.

"I have much to do before nightfall," he declared urgently, "and require your help. I am in need of a quantity of alcohol. Can you know where there is such a liquid?"

Pip was about to say that his request would be diffi-cult to fulfill — she knew one could buy drink in a liquor store, or surgical alcohol from a pharmacy, but the shopkeeper and pharmacist would only sell it to someone over eighteen — when Tim said, "Does it have to be pure alcohol?"

"As pure as possible," Sebastian replied.

"No problemo!" Tim exclaimed, and he made off back towards the house.

"Come," Sebastian invited Pip. "I wish to show you something."

They set off across the rough meadow, the grass seed heads tickling Pip's hands, the dusty smell of pollen making her nose itch.

"Why is this field uneven when the other is flat?" she asked.

"Men have lived in this place for many centuries," Sebastian explained. "Long before my father was given the land, there were houses here. Each of these raised areas is where a building stood, the dips between them ditches or the course of lanes."

A cock pheasant, startled by their approach, suddenly burst into the air almost from their feet, cackling with annoyance. Pip squeaked in alarm and jumped.

"There is no need to be afeared," Sebastian said calmly.

"But what if it was de Loudéac?"

"It will not be."

"How can you be so sure?"

"Because he is away at present."

"How do you know?"

"I just know," Sebastian replied inexplicably, watching the bird glide down, spreading its wings to brake its flight and disappear into the depths of the far hedgerow.

In the center of the field, surrounded by grass so tall that it was invisible even from a short distance away, was a pond. The banks were gently sloping, the water covered in a green carpet of duckweed and water-crowfoot, the edges lined by small bulrushes and a plant that somewhat resembled parsley, but which Pip knew immediately was deadly hemlock.

"This pool," Sebastian announced, "was made by men well before the time of the coming of Our Lord. A tiny spring feeds it from the far side."

"I suppose it was the water supply for the settlement," Pip said.

"No," Sebastian explained. "For that, they went to the river. This pool is a holy place. I will show you."

Sebastian sat down in the long grass, removing his sneakers and rolling his jeans up above his knees. Once barefoot, he slowly stepped into the pool, the duckweed parting before him and closing behind him. Three meters from the bank, he halted, then started to move around very slowly.

"What are you doing?" Pip asked.

"I am feeling with my toes." He stopped and bent down, plunging his arm into the water. When he stood up, duckweed clung to his skin. "I have one," he announced and made for the bank.

"What is it?"

Sebastian placed a small circular disc about two centimeters in diameter and covered in mud in her hand.

"Wash it clean," he said.

Pip knelt at the water's edge and rubbed the object between her finger and thumb. As the mud sluiced off, she saw a silvery pattern of some sort appear.

"What do you see?"

Turning it in her hand, Pip realized it was not a pattern but a head in profile, wearing what resembled a crown of spike-like thorns. Around it was lettering in block capitals.

"It's a coin," she exclaimed, flicking it over to see more writing on the other side, surrounding a figure standing holding what might have been a spear or scepter. She washed it again and the silver became brighter.

"It is a *Roman* coin," Sebastian corrected her.

"Why was it in the pond?" Pip asked.

"To Romans, springs were holy places and they cast money into them as offerings to their gods. And to the Romans, the emperor was a god . . ."

Tim appeared around the coach house, running towards them.

"Here you are," he declared. "Alcohol!" He held out a bottle of vodka.

Sebastian took the bottle, unscrewed the cap and sniffed at it.

"*Aqua vitae!*" he said with obvious glee.

Without saying anything further, he set off in the direction of the river, clutching the bottle as if it were immensely valuable.

"If Dad finds that bottle missing," Pip warned her brother, "you and I are going to be neck deep in serious trouble."

"He won't," Tim said confidently. "When last did you see Mum or Dad drink vodka? He's a scotch-and-water man and Mum drinks gin and tonic. It was only in the drinks cabinet for guests and, anyway, if they can't find it, they'll assume it got lost in the move."

They followed in Sebastian's footsteps, where he had flattened a swathe through the long grass.

"Look what he found in that pond," Pip said, handing the Roman coin to Tim. "That pool was a holy shrine in Roman times. It's full of coins and offerings and things."

"Now that is cool!" Tim replied.

When they caught up with Sebastian, he was striding out, walking at almost a trotting pace.

"Slow down a bit!" Tim said.

Sebastian, who seemed to be walking in a semi-trance, eased up on his pace.

"Can I ask you something?" Pip inquired.

"Certainly."

"How is it that you know so much?" Pip asked. "I mean — you are more or less the same age as us. At least, you are in waking terms. You've never been to school and while your father taught you a lot, I'm sure, he can't have taught you everything you know in just ten years."

"And for the first five years, you must have been just a little sprog anyway," Tim added. He went on, "And some of the stuff you know about, like atomic half-life of elements and such, is knowledge men have only had for the last fifty years or so. And the Human Genome Project's only been going on for a few years, yet you know about it."

"It is simple," Sebastian replied, "for I exist not only here, now, in this time, but also in another."

"Of course!" Tim exclaimed. "Like turning the page."

"Not exactly. I am able to acquire knowledge whilst I am asleep, for then I am able to exist in a parallel universe."

"Run that one by me again," Tim said.

"According to some scientific thought," Sebastian began, "there exist other worlds — other universes — which connect with or relate to our own. These are called parallel universes, which are similar and may even be duplicates of our own, occupied by human beings who are duplicates of ourselves. It is said that we can visit these parallel universes in our sleep and that, when we dream, we are in fact entering one of these other worlds that mimic our own."

"So when you are hibernating, you can go into one of these places?" Pip suggested.

"Yes," Sebastian replied, "and, once there, I can learn, bringing the knowledge with me whither I go."

"Presumably," Tim observed, "de Loudéac can do the same thing."

"Yes," Sebastian said, nodding soberly, "he can."

The ground began to rise slowly. Ahead, half covered in brambles and hawthorn, was a single line of rusty barbed wire strung loosely between fence posts that had rotted through and were either leaning over or held upright only by the wire and the tenacity of the tangle of briars and branches. Behind, on a rise, was a dense clump of trees. Sebastian headed for an almost indiscernible path, holding the barbed wire up for Pip and Tim to duck under.

"This copse is called the Garden of Eden," Sebastian announced, striding past them, pushing the undergrowth aside as he went. "Follow me."

"Isn't this the place the headmaster mentioned?" Tim said under his breath as Pip passed him.

She nodded and set off after Sebastian, Tim a few paces behind her.

After some twenty meters or so, they came upon a clearing in which a large number of different plants was growing, separated by narrow strips of grass.

"It looks like a herb garden gone wild," Pip remarked.

"Which, in a way, is what it is," Sebastian said. "Every plant was originally sown or placed in the ground here by my father. My family have tended them down through the centuries, cultivating them and, where necessary, sowing fresh seed or setting new cuttings. My uncle was the last to honor the responsibility but now, as you can see, it has been abandoned and is in much need of attention."

"I'll do that," Pip offered eagerly. "I like gardening."

Sebastian smiled and said, "That would please me, for I shall have little time for such matters. Furthermore," he added, "you will be safe here, for de Loudéac cannot enter this place to do his mischief."

"Why not?" Tim asked.

"There is much here that can harm him," Sebastian declared, "much that can sap his alchemic strength." He turned to a low plant growing on his right. "Do you know of this?"

Pip squatted next to it. The plant had long, broad leaves that were dark green and deeply ribbed, each of them fanning out from a single point. Three small blue bell-shaped flowers protruded from the center. She rubbed one of the leaves between her fingers and sniffed at them. The smell was awful.

"It is mandragora," Sebastian said, "which protects from evil and demons. This," he pointed to a taller plant whose small mauve flowers were being visited by at least half a dozen wasps, "is figwort, which also protects. And the others here — wormwood, cowbane, selago, oregano, valerian, monkshood . . ."

Setting off around the clearing, Sebastian started to collect a leaf here, a bud or flower there; two plants he uprooted, nipping off tubers, pieces of root or rhizomes before firming them back in the soil with his heel. Each part he collected he pushed into the bottle of vodka, thrusting it down with a green twig snapped from a turkey oak that grew at the edge of the clearing. All the while, he muttered to himself as if casting a spell or reciting a recipe so as not to miss a single ingredient.

When he was done, Sebastian screwed down the cap, shook the bottle vigorously and said, "Now I must prepare my *sauvegarde*."

"*Sauvegarde?*" Tim repeated.

"I think you would call it your safety net," Sebastian replied, shaking the bottle again and setting off towards the edge of the copse.

They returned across the field of rank grass, passing the pool and entering the ruined coach house by squeezing through a half-open door, hanging awkwardly by one hinge. The walls were stained with patches of damp while the upper floor looked unsafe, with gaps where planks had rotted through. The wooden staircase lacked a number of steps and the banister was hanging awry. The flagstoned floor, upon which carriages and dog carts had once stood, was covered in debris, drifts of leaves that had blown in and, against one corner, three or four huge barrels, their bands rusting and their ends staved in. The air smelled of dampness, mold and decaying wood.

Sebastian moved to the middle of the floor and stood upon a large flagstone that seemed more or less devoid of rubbish, beckoning to the others to stand with him. As soon as the three of them were on the stone together, he tapped his foot on two other flags. Immediately, the stone they were standing on appeared to sink into the ground. As it moved downwards, the sides of the shaft sped by. It reminded Tim of being in an old-fashioned elevator where you could see through the bars of the door.

After at least twenty seconds, the feeling of motion ceased and a door opened into Sebastian's underground chamber. Without further ado, he walked straight to the table and poured the contents of the vodka bottle into a glass retort, which he began to connect to a copper distillation tower.

"Is there anything we can do to help?" Pip ventured.

"Nothing," Sebastian replied, "but thank you." He finished setting up his equipment and, with a matchbox, struck a spark and lit a small spirit burner beneath the retort. "And now, I must tell you that I am going away for a few days. You shall not see me, but you need fear not. I shall return before long. In my absence, I must request that you not try to come to this place, for it is protected and those who venture here may only do so in my presence. This is the only means by which I may protect myself whilst I sleep."

"Haven't you ever worried that someone might have found the panel in my bedroom?" Pip asked.

"Or the flagstone in the coach house?" Tim added. "You've been incredibly lucky the builders renovating the house didn't find anything."

"And," Pip added, "if our father decides to convert the coach house into an office, which he is planning to do . . ."

"There is no need to be concerned," Sebastian said. "Were they to dig up the flagstones, they would not find their way here."

"But the shaft . . ." Tim began.

"There is no shaft," Sebastian declared.

"But we just came down it," Tim replied.

"You think you just came down it."

"If there's no shaft," Pip pondered, "where are we? Aren't we under Rawne Barton?"

Sebastian made no answer, but turned his attention to the retort which was now bubbling. The contents were swirling around like vegetables cooking in a boiling saucepan, and steam rose from the surface of the liquid to waft along the tube to the condenser. He watched as a colorless liquid started to drip from the spout into a ceramic dish with a pouring lip on it. He counted the drops. When there were thirty, he extinguished the flame on the burner by covering it with a snuffer and poured the liquid into a dark-blue vial the size of a perfume bottle, which he corked. For a short while, the condenser continued to drip. This liquid he allowed to collect in a small, delicate china vessel rather like an after-dinner coffee cup but with an alchemical symbol drawn on the glaze.

"Now," he said, "I must go."

"Where are you going?" Tim asked.

"I am going," Sebastian said gravely, "in pursuit of evil."

"Can't we come?" Tim asked.

"No," Sebastian said firmly. "This I must do alone for there is much danger and you are not yet ready to face it."

"Is there anything we can do while you're away?" Pip offered.

"Just be on your guard," Sebastian replied, "and," he smiled at Pip, "tend my garden well."

At that, he picked up the cup, put it to his lips, drained it in one swallow and snapped his fingers.

"Yoh! What the . . . !" Tim exclaimed.

The next thing he knew, he found himself standing, holding the bottle of vodka, by the pond in the field, with Pip looking into the water. Of Sebastian there was no sign. However, when Tim looked at the vodka bottle, he noticed that although the top was still on and the seal was unbroken, it was empty.

# Four

## The Edge of Darkness

The following morning, Tim found himself alone in the house. His father, who sometimes worked from a study at home, had gone to London on business. Tim's mother and Pip had departed shortly after him, heading for the county town on what his father termed "a jolly girls' retail-therapy outing," which meant traipsing around department stores trying on clothes that neither of them, in a million years, would dream of buying, never mind wearing.

When he was quite sure everyone had left, Tim went out to the stable block and entered the garage. On a shelf against the back wall was a row of three blue metal toolboxes. Tim searched through them: the first held household tools such as screwdrivers, hammers and chisels, the second electric tools, the third car tools. This he opened wide and started to rummage, lifting out the trays of spanners and wrenches. In the bottom of the box was what he was searching for — a rubber mallet used to knock out dents in the bodywork of cars.

Closing the garage door, he walked towards the coach house, testing the hammer against the palm of his hand as he went. The head was black, solid and heavy, yet it would, Tim knew, serve his purpose ideally. Unlike a metal hammer, whatever he hit with this one would leave no mark.

As he edged himself through the broken door, Tim felt more than a little guilty. He knew he was betraying Sebastian's trust, yet he simply had to know where the allegedly nonexistent shaft was situated.

The coach house looked just as it had when they had entered it the day before, the flagstones littered with leaves, straw and fragments of wood fallen from the floor of the hay loft above. There seemed to be not one flag that had even the faintest sign of having been swept, never mind descending into the bowels of the earth.

Trying hard to remember where they had stood, Tim narrowed it down to one of four large slabs in the center of the coach house. Going down on his hands and knees, he took a deep breath, cast aside his guilty conscience and thumped the hammer on to the flagstone with all his strength. It bounced off. Tim did it again, not so hard, and listened for any sign of an echo, of a dull resonance that might imply a hollow beneath the floor. All that came back was a solid *thonk!*

It was the same with the other three stones. They were, he was sure, set onto bare earth without so much as a drainpipe running beneath them.

Remembering that Sebastian had stood on one flag and tapped two others, Tim tried the same thing, determining that if the stone he was on began to move, he would promptly jump off. That way, he excused himself, he would not upset Sebastian. It was, after all, not as if he wanted to find the chamber, just be assured of the way into it.

Whichever combination he followed, however, nothing happened.

"A virtual shaft," he said out loud to himself. "That's impossible. We went down it. It's not like a computer game. That's virtual. This was . . ." he hated to admit it ". . . actual."

Without disturbing the rubbish lying about unduly, Tim worked his way methodically right across the coach-house floor. Not a single flagstone reverberated.

"Nothing," he muttered. "Plan B."

He put the rubber mallet back where he had found it and, from the household toolbox, picked up a long, thin, flat-headed screwdriver. Armed with this, he crossed the drive to the house, went straight upstairs and entered Pip's room. The flagstones, he reasoned, might have been too thick to allow an echo to pass through, but the panel in Pip's bedroom was not. He had heard that echo, had physically crawled through the paneling and descended into the tunnel.

When Sebastian had first arrived, and just before the paneling swung open, there had been a faint click. This, Tim guessed, was caused by a release mechanism of some sort. All he had to do was to trigger it.

Sitting on the floor before the panel, he remembered that it had swung open on hinges that were on the left side of the panel. The mechanism, he reckoned, must be on the right.

Very carefully, so as not to mark the wood, he tried

to insert the blade of the screwdriver down the side of the panel. It would not go. Although there was a very slight crack, the wood was more or less flush with the panel frame. If he forced it, the wood might splinter or scar, leaving a telltale sign as clear as if he had used a clumsy burglar's jimmy.

What I need, he thought, smiling wryly to himself, is a rubber screwdriver.

Then it came to him. He'd seen it done in films. Hundreds of times.

Going into his own bedroom, Tim opened the drawer of his computer desk and removed his bank cash-machine savings card from his wallet. Returning to Pip's room, he slid it into the gap between the panel and the frame and with difficulty, for it was a tight fit, he slid it up and down the crack. Still nothing. He pushed the card in further, as far as the first raised number of his account. Gripping the card with both hands, he again moved it along the crack.

The click was almost inaudible, but Tim felt the mechanism trip against the card.

"Yes!" he murmured triumphantly.

Using the card as a lever, he edged the panel open. It swung out slowly on its hinges. Behind it, not much more than a centimeter in, was a lath-and-plaster wall.

Like what! he thought.

Tim tentatively tapped the plastic card against the wall. It was firm, hard and doubtless as old as the house itself. There was no indication of a hollow behind it, no sign of even a hairline crack that might indicate a second disguised opening.

He closed the panel and stood up, exasperated and disappointed.

There was no shaft and no tunnel and yet, somehow, he and Pip had followed Sebastian down them.

Back in his bedroom, Tim sat at his desk, replaced the cash card in his wallet and switched on his computer. He resigned himself to the facts. He had been down the tunnel, had been in the underground laboratory — whatever or wherever it was — and he had not been dreaming. There was nothing. No other explanation. Sebastian was on the level. But, and it was a big but, there was a lot — *a lot* — more to him — and parallel universes — than met the eye.

The computer monitor came on, Windows booted up and went immediately into the starfield simulation screen saver. Tim stared at it: it was like flying down a tunnel that was forever opening ahead of him in the center of the screen.

That afternoon, the sun shone through the branches of the trees that grew along the riverbank, dappling the shade. The water was dark yet clear, running over stones here and there or eddying into deep pools on the edge of the current. The banks were steep where the current had cut into them but, where the river ran a straight course, they were gentle and sloped down to the water's edge. It looked tranquil but Tim knew that the currents in such a river could be treacherous, with a dangerous undertow. Certainly, it was not a river for swimming in. Tufts of dry straw hanging from the lower branches of the willows showed him how high the river could flood in the winter.

Choosing a spot where the bank descended gently to a shallow shelf of stones and river gravel, Tim put down his fly rod and landing net and studied the surrounding countryside. Everything seemed in order. There was no one in sight and no black swans either.

Fixing the reel onto his rod, he threaded the line and attached a leader with two droppers, tying on three wet flies — a black butcher, a green nymph and a nondescript brown fly his father had made which he called Dad's Deliverer. In the height of summer, he had discovered, trout could not resist it.

There were trout in the river. Tim could see them swimming by off the end of the shelf, but they seemed not to be feeding. Being within easy casting range of a pool in which at least one was rising regularly, he cast again and again, yet he could not entice it to take a fly. For half an hour he fished in vain before deciding to move upstream.

Passing the knoll, he called out, to be answered by Pip's voice from within the trees. Keeping her promise to Sebastian, she had gone to the clearing straight after returning home. She was trimming the grass, cutting back weeds and pruning any bushes that needed it.

Beyond the knoll, the river ran for about a hundred and fifty meters through meadowland that was a riot of yellow buttercups. On the Rawne Barton side of the river, the bank was broken only by a few trees but, opposite, woodland came right down to the water's edge, the land rising sharply behind the trees to a height of at least sixty meters. Tim could see that a quarry had been cut into this hillside, although it was quite obvious that it had not been worked for many years. In places, creepers hung down the vertical rock slopes, the stone dark and blotched where water ran down it. Wild flowers and bushes had established themselves in some of the crannies. Some way upstream were the stone piers of what had once been a bridge, the arch long since destroyed by time or flood. A flash of brilliant blue across the space between them told him that one of the piers was being used as a perch by a kingfisher.

This, Tim decided, was a good stretch to fish. He knew that where trees hang over the river there would be a large number of insects falling from the leaves into the water. What was more, the river ran deep and dark under the far bank: the deeper and darker it was, the bigger the fish could be. He thought he might even be lucky enough to get a salmon.

On his fourth cast, Tim hooked a large brown trout. No sooner had he struck than it leaped from the water, dived and headed upstream towards a large wych elm growing on the far bank, its roots exposed and arching into the river. Knowing that the fish was heading for the protection of the tangle of submarine roots, Tim fought to turn it, halt its run and bring it back downstream. For three or four minutes, he tussled with the fish before, at last, it began to tire. Gradually, he brought it to the bank and into his landing net.

It was a big fish, weighing well over a kilo, in fine condition. Its back was almost black while its flanks were gray-green with dark-brown and deep-red spots. Holding it still, he hit it on the head with his priest, dispatching it immediately.

"Nice fish!"

Tim jumped, got quickly to his feet and looked around. There was no one in the meadow. Nor was there anyone on the bank. He squinted into the trees, his heart thumping.

"Over 'ere, mate."

The voice was coming from the direction of the wych elm.

"I can't see you," Tim answered, hoping his voice did not betray his fear.

"'Ang on, then," came the reply.

Tim caught a movement in the shadows beneath the trees. Someone was walking down to a point on the bank opposite him. He waited, the branches parted and a young man stepped into view. He was about twenty years old, wearing open-toed sandals, dirty jeans, a T-shirt with a large sunflower printed on it and a very battered black top hat beneath which his hair hung down in dreadlocks.

"You live near 'ere?" he inquired in a friendly voice.

"Yes," Tim confirmed. "In the manor."

"The place they jus' done up?"

"Yes."

"Nice place!"

"Where do you live?" Tim asked, feeling he was volunteering too much information about himself.

The young man jerked his thumb over his shoulder.

"In the quarry," he said. "We got a camp there."

"We?" Tim questioned.

"Me 'n' some mates. Look," he went on, "you don't want to sell your fish, do yer? I'll pay you a coupla quid for it."

"Why don't you catch your own?" Tim said.

"We ain't quite got the knack," the young man admitted. "We been puttin' out night lines with worms 'n' slugs on 'em but all we got so far's an eel."

Tim considered the proposition. His mother still had some trout in the freezer from a fishing trip at Easter — and a "coupla quid" would certainly supplement his pocket money.

"All right," Tim agreed. "I'll sell it to you for £2." He looked at the stretch of deep water between them and the fast current. Wading was out of the question: this was a prime spot for a vicious undertow. And the river was too wide for him to risk throwing the trout over. "How do I get it to you?"

"Walk down the old bridge," the young man said. "It ain't deep where the bridge's fell in."

Collecting up his fishing gear, Tim headed along the bank. As he neared the bridge piers, he saw that the water between them was shallow where large slabs of masonry had formed a natural weir.

"Can yer bring it over?" the young man asked, waving one of his sandaled feet in the air. "I ain't got me boots on." He looked indifferently at the stone bridge abutments. "Been thinkin' of putting a plank across but, well, you know . . ." His voice trailed off.

Leaving his rod and landing net on the bank, Tim picked the trout up, sliding his fingers into its gills, and waded across the river. The current in the center was quick and strong where it ran over the rubble of the bridge but, as the water was shallow, it posed him no problem.

"Here you are." Tim held the fish out. "It's quite heavy."

The young man took it, smiled and said, "I've got the money up in the camp. C'mon up and I'll pay yer."

For a moment, Tim hesitated. How many times, he thought, had he been warned against going off with strangers? His parents, his teachers, the crime prevention officer visiting his school had all pressed home the maxim — *Don't say hello: just go.* Yet this young man seemed innocuous enough: it wasn't as if he was weird or anything, driving an unmarked van and holding out a bag of sweets or offering him a lift home. He was, Tim considered, just a hippy who lived in the woods and, if the worst came to the worst, he could always leg it. Rawne Barton was less than a half a mile away, even if it was on the other side of the river.

Keeping his wits about him, Tim followed the young man along a well-beaten path that wound through the woods in the direction of the quarry face. As they went, he noted landmarks along the way — a rock with a streak of quartz in it, a fallen log, a stand of hazel with the nuts just beginning to swell. If he did have to make a run for it, this would be the way to go.

After a hundred meters or so, the path rounded a bend and opened out into a clearing at the foot of the quarry cliff. There, between massive boulders, were several tents, a distinctly unroadworthy single-decker bus and an equally derelict red van that had, judging by the vague outline of a crown on the side, once been a Royal Mail delivery vehicle. Sitting around a campfire were three other men, two young women dressed in long blouses and skirts to their ankles, and a stark-naked toddler of about two. A nondescript mongrel, which was dozing on its side by the fire, got up on their approach, barked twice in a desultory fashion, wagged its tail half-heartedly, had a good scratch and lay down again.

"Don't mind Woof," said the young man. "Got less bite than bark 'n' not much o' that, neither." He held the fish up. "The boy caught it." He faced Tim. "They call me Splice. You got a name?"

Although he was loath to identify himself to these strangers, Tim gave his name.

"Right, Tim. Take a seat while I get the money."

Splice handed the fish to one of the women and walked off in the direction of the bus. Tim sat down on the nearest boulder to the path, the better to make his escape.

"My name's Filomena," said the young woman with the fish, smiling at him. "And this," she went around the circle of seated hippies, "is Gazer, Reedy, Abby, Dark Horse and Starlight. She's Abby's little girl. We're all Moonbeamers."

"What are Moonbeamers?" Tim asked.

"We are members of the Moonbeam tribe," replied Reedy, a thin man wearing leather trousers and a loose shirt, who looked a few years older than the others. "We are guardians of the moonbeams."

"What he means," explained Gazer, who had a close-shaven head and a silver earring in the shape of a crescent moon hanging from his left lobe, "is that we belong to an organization of those who ride moonbeams."

"Right," Tim said, thinking to himself that they

only rode moonbeams when they were stoned out of their minds.

Splice appeared from the door of the bus and, approaching the fire, flicked a coin to Tim, who caught it.

"Thank you," he said, rising to his feet and pocketing the coin.

"You're welcome to hang loose for a bit," Dark Horse remarked.

"I'd best be getting back," Tim replied, searching for a plausible excuse to leave and conveniently finding it. "I left my fishing rod on the riverbank."

"As you like," commented Dark Horse. *"Do as you will* is the law of the Lord."

"You are welcome here any time you wish," said Filomena, running a sharp, thin-bladed knife down the belly of the fish. Its intestines and carrot-colored roe spilled out onto the earth at her feet.

"Thank you," Tim said again, and he set off down the path.

As he went, he felt their eyes staring at his retreating back. Reaching the bend in the path, he turned and waved, but all he could see was the toddler staggering after him, the fish's guts hanging from her outstretched hands.

Once she had trimmed the grass and begun to tidy up the clearing on the knoll, Pip came to wonder at the amazing diversity of the plants it contained. She had taken her copy of Culpeper's *Herbal* with her and enjoyed identifying the various species that seemed to be growing in distinct plots; none encroached upon the next by more than a matter of centimeters. The perennials were well established, but the annuals and biennials that must have naturally re-seeded themselves had seemingly done so within strictly defined plots, something Pip had never seen before. It was almost as if, even though Sebastian's uncle was long since dead, someone had still been tending to their planting and sowing. Many of the plants Pip already knew without having to look them up — dog mercury, pennyroyal and the figwort which Sebastian had pointed out — but others she had never seen except in books: heart-of-the-earth, fumitory, water pimpernel, galingale and viper's bugloss which had the most exquisite, orchid-like flowers she had ever seen on a wild British plant.

It was idyllic being in the copse. Birds sang and flew over her head or darted from branch to branch. A blackbird with jet plumage and an orange beak that was so bright it looked as if it was made of polished amber sat on a bough in the turkey oak and sang sweetly for minutes at a time, its tune rising and falling, not one sequence of notes repeated. Butterflies and bees visited the flowers and, when she turned over a stone, an almost black toad puffed itself up as if in portly indignation and waddled off to find another safe hiding place. The air filled with the scent of blossom and, when she brushed against an aromatic leaf, its perfume wafted over her. The only sound or sight of any other human was Tim briefly calling out as he passed on his way up the river and, later, when she spied him in the distance talking to someone on the other bank.

Although Sebastian had said as much, she felt utterly

safe on the knoll. The woods, like woodland anywhere, had a timeless quality to them.

For nearly two hours Pip worked with her attention undivided, and by five o'clock she felt she had done as much as she dared. Conscious that this place was not only special but also of vital importance to Sebastian, she was reluctant to do too much without his agreement. Standing at the edge of the clearing, she surveyed what she had achieved. The passageways through the plants were now tidy and well defined, the grass short. Where surrounding trees had started to grow over plants at the clearing's edge, they were cut back. Satisfied that she had achieved all she had set out to, and placing the herbal and gardening tools in her basket, Pip set off for the house.

Just as she was about to lift up the strand of barbed wire at the edge of the wood, Pip had the uneasy feeling that someone — or something — was watching her. She paused, still partially hidden in the shade of the copse.

Pip could see as far as the coach house, where she could just make out Tim turning the corner, his rod and landing net over his shoulder. She watched him disappear and began to scan the field. It was empty, no other person in sight. Yet, she thought, the grass was long — anyone could be crouching in it. Backtracking a short way, she came upon a sycamore tree. The lowest boughs were within reach so she dropped her basket and swung herself up, climbing from branch to branch to a height of about five meters. From this vantage point, she could see down into the meadow. Nothing was concealed anywhere in the grass.

Collecting her basket, Pip left the copse and set off across the field, keeping to the center as much as possible, as far away as she was able from the hedges. If, she reasoned, someone were to come after her, she would see them in good time and take to her heels.

As she reached the middle of the field, Pip felt confident — then it occurred to her. At this point she was the farthest from either the safety of the house or that of the copse. Suddenly, she felt nervous and glanced over her shoulder.

Along the edge of the copse, a faint mist was rising from the grass. It was not gray, as if it were water vapor or smoke, but seemed to be marbled with many different, indefinable colors. It hovered for a moment, then began to drift in her direction.

She started to walk quickly towards the house, not daring to look back, not wanting to risk breaking into a run for fear of tripping and falling.

Suddenly, Pip was struck a glancing blow on the top of her head. Her hair was firmly tugged. Something sharp hit her scalp. Dropping her basket, she instinctively raised her arms to defend herself. A moment passed, then something soft brushed her hands. She looked up. It was the blackbird.

Banking high above her, it turned again and dived, its twig-like feet coming at her with its talons spread like a bird of prey's. Snatching at her hair, it tore a tuft free, rising into the air, shrilling its *pink-pink-pink* alarm call.

Casting all caution aside, Pip started to run. But the bird did not repeat its attack. Instead, it flew in circles in the sky above her.

Pip had not gone ten steps when her foot was

snagged by a tussock of tangled grass. She stumbled, but kept going.

In her ears, there grew a hissing noise. At first she thought it was the sound of the long grass brushing against her jeans, but it increased in volume and pitch until it seemed to fill her head.

Out of the blue, the air was filled with a maelstrom of insects — butterflies, bees, gnats, grasshoppers, mosquitoes, dragonflies, wasps, lacewings and shield bugs. They beat against her face, crawled over her neck, tangled themselves in her hair and sought to get in her mouth, nostrils and ears. A large beetle at least two centimeters long hit her hard in the throat and fell inside her T-shirt. She could feel its spiny legs scrabbling for purchase on her flesh, the plates of its carapace trying to close over its wings.

Screaming, Pip ran headlong towards the coach house, which was now just a blur through the insect blizzard. She flailed her arms about her, but in vain. Still they came, their wings obscenely stroking her, their legs sickeningly scratching at her skin. When they started to bite and sting, Pip slapped at herself, feeling their tiny bodies explode to release a putrid stink of insect blood and bile.

Then, as quickly as it had appeared, the insect swarm simply vanished. Pip found herself at the corner of the coach house, her head reeling, her fingers sticky and the beetle moving inside her clothing.

Tearing her T-shirt out of her jeans, she held it taut away from her body. The insect tumbled heavily onto the ground at her feet, its reddish-brown wing cases polished, the rear end of its abdomen grotesquely pointed, its thorax black and furry-looking with antennae like minuscule fans.

Lifting her foot, Pip was about to stomp on the creature when it opened its wing cases and with a loud buzzing clumsily took off to fly over the coach house and out of sight.

Still shaking, Pip went to the garden tap by the stables and rinsed the remains of the insects from her hair, face and arms.

"Insects!"

"Yes," Pip said, annoyed at Tim's reaction. "Insects. Every insect you could name."

"All together?"

"I've already told you."

"So dragonflies that usually eat other insects, and wasps that often attack bumblebees, were all flying in the same cloud?"

"What else do you want me to say? Yes!"

"Makes no sense," Tim said.

"I don't care if it makes sense or not. They did it. Maybe it was like when there's a forest fire and the lions run with the antelopes . . ."

"You saw a fire?" Tim asked sarcastically.

Pip reached for her T-shirt where it lay over her dressing-table seat. "Here!" She tossed it over to her brother. It was besmirched with spots and smears of green, yellow and dull crimson. "Look at the stains!

You see a felt-tip pen?" she said, returning his sarcasm. "That's designer insect."

"OK!" Tim replied. "It happened. But why? What did you do? I mean, if you kick over a beehive, the bees gang up and go for you. Or a wasp nest. But every insect . . ."

"And the blackbird," Pip reminded him. "That came straight at me. A laser-guided bomb wouldn't have been more accurate. And it tore a chunk of my hair out."

Tim grinned and said, "Don't worry, it doesn't show." He picked up the T-shirt and sniffed at it. "Like the designer insect perfume." He held the garment against himself. "We could start a whole new fashion trend with this. The squashed-insect motif. Armani and Gucci, here we come."

Pip, who was beginning to lose her temper with Tim, saw the funny side and laughed.

"The thing is," Tim went on, "why you?"

Shrugging, Pip said, "I don't know."

"You say you were in the copse for at least two hours."

"At least. I was already there when you went by with your rod, and later on I saw you talking to someone across the river. Who was that? Another fisherman?"

"No. A hippy," Tim replied. "There's a camp in the woods there. Well, three tents, an old bus and a van. Four men, two women, a flea-ridden mutt and a snotty little kid. They bought a big trout I landed." He paused, then went on, "Did you do anything in the clearing that might have disturbed the insects?"

"Like what? All I did was a bit of pruning and cutting. Nothing bothered me. There were insects there — butterflies and bees on the flowers, grasshoppers, ants. A blackbird singing . . ."

She stopped in mid-sentence and looked at Tim. He looked at her.

"'You will be safe here because de Loudéac cannot enter this place,'" they chorused.

"But the minute you step outside that barbed wire, you're fair game," Tim said. "And you say the insects vanished the minute you reached the coach house?"

"Yes."

"That must mean that the house and its surroundings are safe too. Maybe because Sebastian lives here. Maybe his father put a protective spell on the place. Whatever."

"What about the stinging butterfly?" asked Pip, remembering the insect that had bitten her on her first night at Rawne Barton.

For a moment, Tim was silent.

"Maybe," he said at length, "it wasn't a butterfly. Maybe that was a genuine mistake . . ."

"It was a butterfly!" Pip snapped. "And I was in the garden. Close to the house."

Tim tried to explain it away. "Maybe it only looked like a butterfly. Some insects mimic others for their own protection. Knowledge gained courtesy of the National Geographic channel."

"Tim! It sucked my blood."

"But you said the bite soon vanished. Maybe it wasn't a bite. Maybe it was an allergic reaction. Some caterpillars bring you out in a rash, so . . ."

"National Geographic?" Pip asked, ironically.

"No. That was from watching the BBC Natural History Unit."

Pip looked out of her bedroom window. The evening was drawing in. From downstairs the mouth-watering aroma of roast chicken wafted up.

"I've just thought," Pip said with a tremble in her voice, turning from the window, "if the wood and the house are safe, that means that everywhere else is *un-safe*."

"Not necessarily," Tim replied. "What about this. You've only been attacked when you've been alone. Nothing's happened when I have been around. What's more, if the insects attacked you in the field, why didn't they attack me too? I was alone."

"Until you met the Weirdos of Quarry Wood. Maybe you met the hippy just as the insects were gathering to attack you, but you didn't notice because you were concentrating on your fishing."

"No," Tim said. "I'd've noticed." He stood up. "We'd better go down. Supper must be about on the table." He moved to the door and held it open for his sister to go ahead of him.

"So polite!" she remarked sardonically.

"Not at all," Tim answered. "If there's a python on the stairs, it'll get you first."

Pip gave her brother a filthy look.

"Sorry!" he apologized. "But seriously, I think from now on you don't go anywhere outside the immediate vicinity of the house unless you're accompanied by someone. Me. Mum or Dad. Sebastian. Whoever. Agreed?"

Pip nodded. This was not, she thought, turning into the kind of summer she had planned.

The following day, the summer weather that had lasted since before the house move finally broke, replaced by a day of somber skies and squally showers. Pip spent the morning in her room, listening to CDs and reading a file of printouts Tim had downloaded from an Internet site. It had lots of information about the alchemical properties and uses of herbs and gemstones.

It was, she discovered, amazing how magical attributes were credited to so many plants and minerals. Cloves could be used to exorcise spirits, a common broom protected against evil, the ash tree resisted magical forces and purslane aided in the detection of illusions. As for minerals, amber could make a woman confess her sins, diamonds would go dark in the presence of guilt or evil, while a lotion of amethyst guarded against witchcraft.

Thumbing through the pages, a small but indistinct picture caught her eye. Removing the page from the file, she left her room and went into Tim's. He was bending over the keyboard of his computer with a joy-stick to one side, engrossed in Flight Simulator, a not uncommon sight.

"What are you doing?" she asked.

"Landing an Airbus 300 at Boston Logan," Tim replied.

Pip, knowing he hated to be interrupted, watched

over his shoulder as the aircraft turned; she could see the runway in the distance through the virtual cockpit window, the approach lights drawing nearer. Tim, turning from keyboard to joystick, held his course, increasing the flap angle and slowing himself by lowering the undercarriage. As soon as the aircraft touched down, he paused the game.

"Tim," Pip asked, now that Tim and his passengers were safely on the runway, "have you kept the pages you gave me on hard disk?"

"Every one," he confirmed. "As HTML files."

"Can you call one up?" She held out the page.

Tim called up Windows Explorer and double-clicked on the folder, then on the file.

"Blow that picture up," she requested.

Tim opened Paint Shop Pro and did as he was told. As the picture appeared, filling the screen, Pip sucked in her breath.

"What's up, sis?"

"That flower," Pip said, pointing to the screen, "grows in the garden. I found it just before the butterfly stung me. If you sniff the flower, it makes you instantly dizzy."

"What do you mean?"

"Just that. The flower's huge — at least twenty centimeters long. When I sniffed at it, I got all giddy. Go back to the file."

Tim returned to the HTML file, clicked on Print and, when the printer had produced the page, read the text out loud.

"*Brugmansia grandiflora*, the Angel's Trumpet. Perennial evergreen originally from South America, may grow as high as 3.5 meters. Large hairy leaves, pendulous white trumpet blooms which usually last only one day. Prefers partial shade or partial sun and moist soil. Hardy to 20 to 25°F or -7 to -5°C. Poisonous. Known to be used in Native American rituals, the powdered seeds mixed with corn beer. Was used in Europe in the Middle Ages mixed with wine or beer; was considered an ingredient of 'flying ointment' used by witches and facilitated shape-shifting." He scrolled up the page. "Flying ointment?" he exclaimed. "Shape-shifting? What's that?"

"I shall show you."

Pip spun round. Tim almost fell off his computer-desk chair. Standing behind them was Sebastian.

"I have returned," he announced unnecessarily, closing the door behind him, "and I must speak urgently with you."

"Where have you been?" Pip asked.

Sebastian sat on Tim's bed, leaning forward. He looked tired and wan.

"I have been walking in the footsteps of evil," he said matter-of-factly, without any sense of drama. "I have been to the edge of darkness. And you, I believe," he glanced up at Pip, "have been not far behind me."

"I was attacked by insects," Pip said.

"And a blackbird," Sebastian added.

"Yes." Pip was surprised he knew. "It tore my hair out."

"It was de Loudéac, or his ally," Sebastian declared, "yet I dared not intervene for I did not wish him to know of my whereabouts. I am sorry."

"Where were you?" Tim asked.

"I was nearby," Sebastian said evasively, "unseen but

all-seeing. I was there as you caught your fish, as you crossed the river to meet with Splice, as you walked to the quarry, as you returned."

For a moment, Tim cast his mind back to that afternoon, then said, "You were the kingfisher."

Sebastian gave a brief but knowing smile before his face became serious once more.

"De Loudéac is striving greatly to achieve his end. I know not where he is conducting his experiments, but it is surely not far off. He is seeking possession."

"Possession of what?" Pip ventured.

"At present, possession of anything that might aid him."

"Such as insects?" Tim suggested.

Sebastian nodded gravely and said, "The insect vortex was one such possession."

"But why is he going after me?" Pip asked.

"As yet I know not," Sebastian admitted. "It may be that he knows you are in league with me and, therefore, regards you as his enemy. Perhaps, because you live in my father's house, he believes you are for us."

"For us?" Tim queried.

"On our side, in support of our cause."

"You'd better believe it!" Tim replied, grinning.

Sebastian glanced at the printout on the desk. "I see you have discovered the *herbe aux sorciers* — the sorcerer's plant."

"There's one growing in the garden," Pip said.

"As with many other plants hereabouts, my father planted it. At his trial, it was used as evidence against him, for it was said that one who partook of the plant danced with the devil."

"What about all this flying ointment and shape-shifting?" Tim said.

"The plant contains powerful poisons called alkaloids," Sebastian replied, ignoring Tim's request for an explanation. "Consumed by the unwitting, they can be very dangerous, stimulating the nervous system but depressing peripheral nerves such as those in the hands or feet. A man partaking of these poisons turns into a fool and may remain thus thereafter, lingering between sanity and insanity, between joy and sorrow, even between life and death, until the day when Our Lord shall call him to His presence. The plant is an ingredient of my father's *aqua soporiferum*, for it relaxes the muscles of the chest and lungs. You see, in the hands of the skilled alchemist . . ." He paused, as if reluctant to speak further on the subject.

"You've still got to say what flying ointment is and . . . ." Tim replied.

"Shape-shifting," Sebastian said. "Observe!"

Sebastian pressed his two index fingers together and blew hard through the space between them, producing a brief, high-pitched squeak. Pip and Tim stood watching him. Waiting a few moments, he repeated the action.

"Thus come the tiny creatures," he stated, and pointed to the skirting board under Tim's window.

Close to the woodwork was a field mouse, hunched down with its whiskers quivering, its tail wrapped round its side.

"The Pied Piper of Rawne Barton!" exclaimed Tim.

"Quite so," Sebastian said. "It is possible, if one knows how, to call up any creature, for one has only to know its limited vocabulary."

91

"And what did you say in mouse-speak?" Pip asked.

"I cannot know. But this sound always calls them hither. Now," Sebastian stood up, snapped his fingers and went down on his haunches, "watch the mouse. Do not take your mind from it."

Pip and Tim gave the mouse their undivided attention. For a moment, it was just a timid mouse crouching against the wall, but then, gradually, it started to change both size and shape.

"Wow!" Tim whispered in awe. "It's . . . it's becoming . . ." His eyes were wide with amazement. "Do you see it, sis?"

"Yes," Pip said, her voice filled with wonder.

The mouse was now at least four times as big as it had been, its tail was thicker and longer and it had changed color from dull gray to a dark, glossy brown. Its whiskers had grown to at least four times their previous length and its eyes, which had been barely visible, were now jet-black beads set in its inquisitive face. The tiny mouse ears were now not only larger but, instead of being set flush against the side of its head, were pricked up and listening.

"That's wicked!" Tim said, bending over. "Come here . . ."

At the sound of his voice, the mouse turned its head and looked straight at him. The tip of its tail flicked once.

Sebastian snapped his fingers. In an instant, the mouse went back to being a plain mouse and ran for cover, vanishing down a slim crack in the floorboards.

"That was awesome!" Tim exclaimed. "How did you do it?"

"I did not," Sebastian answered. Then, turning to Pip, he asked, "What did you see?"

"What did I see?" Pip replied. "Well, it was a mouse, but then it changed into the most beautiful rat I've ever seen."

"Rat?" Tim exploded.

"Yes, rat."

"Sis," Tim said, with more than a hint of exasperation, "it was a cat. Brown, long tail, whiskers, perky ears."

"It was both," Sebastian interrupted. "The mouse itself did not change. It was a mouse all the while. What altered was your perception of it."

"Look," Tim said, "I might be as thick as an elephant omelette, but I think I know the difference between a cat and a rat."

"Of course," Sebastian agreed, "but you saw what you wanted or expected to see. Thus it is with shape-shifting."

"So," Pip said, "shape-shifting is not a matter of actual transformation, but . . ." she sought for a way to explain her thoughts ". . . of somehow making us think we see something. Like hypnotizing us."

"In a manner of speaking," Sebastian replied. "It is more a method of manipulating your emotions and thoughts."

"So," Tim reasoned, "what you're saying is that when Pip was dive-bombed by a blackbird, it was really de Loudéac who made her think he was a blackbird."

"Precisely!" Sebastian declared. "He makes you see something else so that he may draw near to you unobserved — or, rather, unrecognized. It is but a way of being invisible."

All that evening, the rain lashed against the windows. After supper, the family sat in the living room. Tim and his father were watching highlights from the previous weekend's motor racing on TV while Pip read and her mother did some sewing.

Despite herself, Pip could not concentrate on her book. Her mind kept wandering and she found herself repeatedly thinking of Sebastian's father's trial, which had been held in this very room. Every time she looked over at her mother, sitting in an armchair by the huge inglenook fireplace, Pip thought of Sebastian's father seated in exactly the same place, facing his accusers, who occupied chairs where the Sony digital television now stood. And de Loudéac, she thought, had he been where she was now, watching his enemy beginning his inexorable descent into the flames of the execution pyre? The panels around the walls, the heavy, carved oak beams holding up the ceiling, the frame of the door, the stone mantelshelf over the fireplace: they had all witnessed the trial. She wondered if, in the deepest atoms of the stone and wood, there still lingered the slightest sound wave of the words spoken and if, one day far into the future, someone would develop the technology to pick up those words and replay them.

At ten-thirty, the lights in the living room were extinguished and the family went up to bed. Mr. Ledger had to leave before breakfast the following morning for a business meeting and wanted to get an early night. Pip went up to her room and, after a shower, got into bed and went to sleep.

Tim, not feeling tired, sat at his computer desk, went into his ISP and read an e-mail from a friend at his last school. He replied to it, logged off, booted up Flight Simulator and prepared to fly a Boeing 777 from London Heathrow to Rome Leonardo da Vinci, in real time. He chose the Delta Airlines livery, plotted his route and lined up at the end of runway 27L. Lightly holding his joystick, he throttled up the engines, released the brakes and began to roll. In twenty minutes, he was over the French coast near Caen, at his initial cruising altitude of nine-thousand meters. The waypoints set, he put the jet into auto pilot and sat back watching the virtual French countryside sliding by, the clouds far below but some high-altitude cover coming up. If, he thought, he was a real pilot, he would now be putting on the seat-belt warning light and instructing the cabin director to tell the passengers to return to their seats because they were in for a little turbulence.

With no necessity to be in the cockpit for another thirty-five minutes, when he would need to fly over the Alps near Grenoble and enter Italian airspace, Tim stood up, undressed, put on his pajamas and went to the bathroom to brush his teeth. Returning to his room, he checked the flight data — the aircraft had just altered course at a radio beacon over Tours — and went to the window to draw the curtains. The rain was beating against the glass, carried on a stiff wind.

As he pulled one curtain across to meet the other, the glint of a pinprick of greenish light caught Tim's eye. At first, he thought it was the power diode on his computer reflected in the window, but it was not. It was outside.

Opening the window against the torrential rain and wind, he saw it again. It seemed to be winking, like the eye of a predator caught in the beam of a headlight. And it was coming from the direction of the copse on the knoll.

"Pip!" Tim hissed, drumming his fingers lightly on her bedroom door. "Pip!"

"What?" came the drowsy reply.

He opened the door and asked, "Pip! Are you awake?"

"No, I'm fast asleep," Pip retorted, sitting up and reaching for her bedside light.

"Leave it off," Tim said quietly, closing the door behind him. "Come and look at this."

He went to her window and pulled aside a curtain. Pip stood beside him, rubbing her eyes.

"What?"

"Over there, in the trees by the river."

She peered into the darkness. The green light flashed off and on.

Immediately, she was wide awake. "What is it?"

"Like I know?" said Tim. "I only just saw it." He let the curtain fall and switched on the bedside light. "We've got to tell Sebastian."

"Yes," Pip agreed, then she paused. "How? We've never contacted him. He's always got in touch with us."

"Knock on the paneling," Tim suggested, and he knelt by his sister's bed, tapping very gently on the wood. He hoped it might echo, that somehow the tunnel was there after all, not just the lath-and-plaster wall. His knock, however, was not met with any resonance. He tried again. In vain.

"Maybe we could go out to the coach house," Pip suggested, regretting it the moment the words were out of her mouth. The last thing she wanted to do was leave the security of the house.

"No point," said Tim, without admitting how he knew. "If he isn't here, he isn't going to be there. Maybe," he added, "the light's his."

They heard a soft footstep outside Pip's door. A cat's paw would not have made such a faint sound. A floorboard creaked.

"Tim . . . ," Pip whispered. She reached for Tim's hand and gripped it so tightly his fingers hurt.

There was another step. Someone was making their way along the corridor on tiptoe. Or something.

"What do we do?" Pip mumbled, her mouth going dry.

Tim shrugged and looked around the room. Against the wall was Pip's tennis racket. He removed his hand from hers and, picking it up, positioned himself beside the door. It was not, he admitted to himself, much of a weapon. His bat would have been more effective but that was in the wardrobe in his room.

The steps halted outside the door. There was a snuffling sound, as if a dog were running its nose along the bottom of the door. A scratching at the door was followed by the handle beginning to turn. Pip hid behind her bed. She wanted to scream but, instead, pressed her hands over her ears as if not hearing what was outside would somehow cause it not to exist.

Raising the racket over his head, Tim held his breath. The door opened. Four fingers covered in fur, like those of a bizarre ape, the nails small, the skin wrinkled and black with the ends blunt and grimy, appeared round the edge. Tim wondered if he should smash the racket down now or wait a moment until he saw the creature's head.

"Pip," came a barely audible but gruff voice. "Tim."

As he looked, Tim saw the fingers beginning to lose their hair, the black skin turning ashen.

"Pip, Tim. Are you there?" The voice was marginally less gruff. "It is I."

Tim lowered the racket. Sebastian entered the room. His hands, and everything else about him, were quite normal.

"Your hands . . . ." Tim began, then he realized. "Were you shape-shifting?"

Sebastian smiled and said, "I am sorry, Tim. What you saw was what you did not want to see."

"Like, what?" Tim exclaimed.

"To put it another way," Sebastian added, "what you saw was what you were afraid to see. I regret that I may have influenced your imagination through the door."

"You mean, hypnotized us?" Tim suggested.

Sebastian answered, "In a manner of speaking," and nodded in the direction of the window. "You too have espied the light, have you not?"

"Yes," Tim replied.

Going to the other side of Pip's bed, where she was still hunched up, her hands to her ears and her eyes screwed shut, Tim touched her on the shoulder. She jumped as if someone had just shocked her.

"It's okay. It's Sebastian."

Pip got up, feeling a little sheepish.

"Be not ashamed," Sebastian said. "Fear comes to us all and we each deal with it in our own way." He parted the curtains and glanced out. "The light remains and I must go forth to discover its cause."

"We'll come too," Pip announced, hoping to regain some of her self-esteem and vowing never again to hide in the face of whatever might come.

Five minutes later, the house alarm system deactivated, they crept out of the kitchen door and, heading across to the coach house, paused before setting off across the field.

"Stay close," Sebastian ordered unnecessarily. "If we are as one, de Loudéac will think twice before acting upon us."

As they stepped around the corner of the coach house, the wind struck them hard, momentarily stealing their breath away. The rain pelted their faces. Despite wearing fleeces with the necks buttoned tight, the rain seeped inside quickly, running down their backs and chilling them. The tossing grass thrashed their legs. In less than thirty meters, their jeans were soaked through, their feet sodden in their sneakers.

Halfway to the knoll, the field became waterlogged. Although the river had not burst its banks, the water table had risen, turning the field into a temporary grassy swamp. Their progress was heavy going; the only light they had to guide themselves by was that in the copse and the faint glow reflecting off the clouds from Brampton, a few miles away.

At the strand of barbed wire, Sebastian stopped and

said, "Whatever you see, or hear, remember it is but an image in your head. No harm can befall you for you will be within the protection of the Garden of Eden." With that, he held up the wire and stepped beneath it.

Pip followed, Tim taking up the rear. Very cautiously, they moved in single file through the trees. The wind blew hard in the boughs above them, tossing branches about and shedding small twigs that fell upon them as they advanced through the covert. Reaching the clearing, the pathways that Pip had cleared and trimmed stood out before them. In the very center, hanging from a Y-shaped staff stuck in the earth, was an ancient cast-iron lantern. The flame within it glowed a delicate green, flickering as the wind licked at the lamp's chimney.

"Why it is green, not orange?" Pip whispered.

"De Loudéac has added powdered antimony to the oil," Sebastian explained, keeping his voice low.

"What is antimony?" Tim asked softly.

"It is a metal, ruled by fire, which an alchemist called Basil Valentine discovered would act against men of holy inclination. Hence its name, for antimony derives from the Latin, meaning *against a monk*. Mixing it with the lamp oil makes for a devilish light."

With that, Sebastian stepped into the clearing, raising his arms as a priest might before an altar.

*"In nomine patris omnipotentis, domine sancta, eterne deus, tu fecisti coelum et terram,"* he intoned, walking towards the lamp, *"discedo, defluo, abeo . . ."*

For a moment, nothing happened; then, from the far side of the clearing, there rose a black shadow darker than the night. It swept towards Sebastian, swirling above him like a miniature tornado. The smell of burning hair filled the wind. Pip felt it snatching at her throat. Tim, at her side, coughed loudly.

Sebastian did not move. He stood quite still with his arms raised. The narrow base of the black tornado sought him out, pulling at his clothes, which whipped about him.

"We've got to do something!" Pip exclaimed, choking on the stench.

Sebastian was being lifted from the ground, his feet a good few centimeters above the grass. He was beginning to spin with the force of the whirlwind.

Side by side, Pip and Tim ran forward, yelling at the tops of their voices. The tornado seemed to waver. The wide top of its funnel bent towards them as a face might upon suddenly seeing them. For a few seconds, it moved in their direction, carrying Sebastian with it. A meter from them, it halted and, with a piercing whistle, it rose rapidly into the air, dissipating as it hit the blast of the storm blowing over the treetops.

"I am indebted to you," Sebastian said, dizzy from being spun round and trying to stand upright. "De Loudéac would not have won this petty joust, but that was not his intention. You might say he was flexing his muscles as best he could, to deter me from my mission."

"He might have killed you," Pip said, putting her hand on Sebastian's shoulder to steady him.

"No," Sebastian replied. "He could lift me no higher."

"I thought he couldn't come into this wood," Tim stated.

"He may enter," Sebastian replied, "as he did when

Pip was tending the plants, yet he may do little harm here. His powers are much reduced within the precinct of the wood."

"What was he doing here?" Pip pondered aloud.

Sebastian pointed to the figwort growing close by and said, "Look, you can see where I picked a flower head when we were in this place together. And here, where I took a leaf of valerian. See how this other leaf has been torn? De Loudéac was in this place, seeking to copy my *sauvegarde*."

"What does he want to do that for?" Tim asked.

"If he could copy it," Sebastian said, "he could the better counteract my magic and attack me." At that point, he laughed. "Yet he is confused. He came here to study which plants I had used but you, Pip, have been here since with your pruning implements. Now, he cannot tell which plants I cut and which you."

He walked across to the lantern, opening it. The wind extinguished the flame immediately. No sooner was it out than both the lantern and the staff melted into thin air.

"We must be gone," Sebastian announced, "and you must return home, for the dampness will give you the ague unless you warm yourselves."

"You'll catch cold as well," Pip said, but Sebastian seemed not to hear her and started striding out of the wood.

Pip and Tim followed him across the field. At the coach house, Sebastian waved to them and entered the building as they returned to the main house. They let themselves in and, resetting the alarm, silently went up to their rooms.

When Tim reached his bedroom, he found his Delta Airlines flight to Rome within ten minutes of landing but three hundred miles off course. He hit the Esc key and, undressing, started to towel himself dry.

Why play at being an airline pilot, he thought, when he was living in a real-life equivalent of *Tomb Raider*?

# Five

# The Shout

The storm had gone by dawn, leaving the country-side bathed in brilliant summer sunlight. Mrs. Ledger announced at breakfast that she was going to spend the morning investigating Brampton and, as she put it, get her bearings on the butcher, the baker and the candlestick maker.

"Have a good time," Tim said, tipping his cereal bowl to get the last of the milk and muesli onto his spoon.

"I'm sure we will," his mother responded.

It was a moment before Tim caught the significance of the reply.

"We?"

"Yes, 'we,'" said his mother. "You and Pip are coming too. We have to register with the doctor and the dentist."

And so, just after nine o'clock, they left Rawne Barton in Mrs. Ledger's car for the nearby town.

"How do you like living here?" their mother asked as she negotiated the narrow country lanes, having to pull in to let first a tractor, then a milk-collecting truck squeeze past.

"It's cool," said Tim, noncommittally.

Both he and Pip knew that when their mother started asking questions like that out of the blue, she was not just making conversation, but was on a mission of discovery.

"The house is wonderful," Pip added.

"Yes, isn't it?" Mrs. Ledger replied. "Just think of all that has gone on in our own home, right back down through history."

And you don't know the half of it, thought Tim.

"And the countryside is beautiful," Pip remarked.

"It certainly is. When I was a little girl, you used to still see fields of wildflowers, but then they died out. Farming methods changed. Nowadays, you only see wildflowers in National Trust places and SSSIs. But our back field, behind the coach house — that's a wonder to behold."

"What's an SSSI?" Tim asked, hoping to take some control of this seemingly innocuous conversation.

"A site of special scientific interest," his mother told him. "A government classification for land that cannot be disturbed — dug up, plowed, built upon, sprayed with chemicals."

Halting at a T-junction, Mrs. Ledger waited for a delivery van to pass. The signpost indicated Brampton to the left and Stockwold to the right. She turned left.

"Your friend Sebastian seems a pleasant boy," she remarked as the car accelerated.

So, Tim thought, that was where this camouflaged interrogation was heading.

"Yes," Pip said, exchanging a glance with her brother. "He's really nice. Can we have him to stay over one night?"

Sharp move, Tim considered. His sister was no fool. Get their mother on the back foot . . .

"Of course," Mrs. Ledger said. "Do you . . . ?"

"He is going to go to Bourne End Comprehensive too," Pip went on, justifying the lie: after all, if Sebastian were to attend any school, that would probably be the one — and he had once gone to a local school. "He'll be in the same year as us but I don't know what class."

"I think he's good at science," Tim chipped in, "so he might be in a top set."

"I hope you two will be as well," their mother retorted. "Is he . . . ?"

"And he's very good at history," Pip continued. "He knows all about the history of our house, when it was built and everything."

"I'm going fishing again this afternoon," Tim announced, changing the subject to get it away from Sebastian before his mother could respond. "There's a really neat stretch where the trees overhang the water."

They reached the outskirts of Brampton. The sides of the road were so jammed with parked cars, passing traffic was at a crawl. There was a line ten cars long to get into the town parking lot.

"It's very busy!" Mrs. Ledger exclaimed, with more than a hint of concern in her words. "I thought this would be a sleepy little place."

Tim winked at Pip. She grinned back. Their mother, who always got flustered when driving in traffic, would not be of a mind now to delve further into the mystery of Sebastian.

As they turned into the high street, the reason for the traffic was explained. It was market day. The street was lined with stalls on the pavements selling anything from cheap clothing to fresh fish, fruit and vegetables, from locally made farmhouse cheeses and second-hand books to a wide variety of bread baked with organic flour. What was throughout the rest of the week a quiet little country town was now a bustling hive of activity: farmers meeting to discuss agricultural matters, house-wives chattering as they shopped, stallholders calling out their wares, the occasional tourist wandering about photographing what was to them an old English scene, unchanged for eons.

With some difficulty, Mrs. Ledger managed to park near the doctor's office and they went in just in time for their appointment. Dr. Oliver was a young man with incredibly long fingers and, Pip thought, sad eyes. He told them he was a local man, requested that they fill out registration forms and asked if they had any current medical conditions or problems.

"Only Pip," Mrs. Ledger started. "She has a small wart on her left thumb. Our last doctor was going to remove it, but then we moved . . ."

Dr. Oliver took Pip's hand, looked at the wart and said, "That's no problem at all. I can take it off in a day or two. Do make an appointment as you go out."

Leaving the office, they walked in the direction of the high street.

"I'm going to look around the market," Mrs. Ledger announced.

"We would never have guessed," Tim said.

"And I suppose it goes without saying . . . ." their mother began. Then she added, "Be back at the car in an hour."

"Time to kill," Tim said, somewhat despondently.

He did not want to hang around the market and there were no shops in the street he wished to visit. Apart from a greengrocer, a butcher, a pharmacy, a mini-mart, a hairdresser, a post office, a hardware store that advertised repairs to lawnmowers and a tea shop called Ye Olde Cream Bunne, there was precious little else.

"I've an idea," Pip declared. "You coming?"

Tim shrugged and followed his sister as she set off across the street, weaving through the market stalls, the sauntering throng of shoppers and the slow-moving traffic. At the entrance to an alley quaintly called The Snuck, she paused to get her bearings then made her way down it. At the end, they came out into a small cobbled square in front of the thirteenth-century church. A noticeboard by the ancient lych-gate announced in gold paint:

*The Church of Saint Benedict and the*
*Blessed Raymond Lull*
*Rector: The Rev. Eric Crane*

Pip pushed open the gate and entered the graveyard. A gravel path led up to the church porch.

"Tim," Pip said, "go in the church and have a look at the monuments on the wall and the graves set into the floor."

"And look for what?"

"You'll know when you see it," she answered enigmatically and, stepping off the path, began to walk slowly along the first row of ancient headstones.

Entering the church, Tim worked his way around the building, studying every monument. Those on the walls were mostly dedicated to notable locals who had died since about 1750: there was a sea captain who was lost overboard from an East Indiaman in the South China Sea in 1793 and a Dr. Artemus Drage who, in 1821, had invented a clockwork astrolabe. Most of the gravestones set into the floor of the aisle were worn smooth by the feet of worshippers. The only tomb was set into an alcove in the choir and had upon it an alabaster figure of a man in Elizabethan court dress, a sword at his side and a ruff at his throat. His nose, the toes of his shoes and the fingers of one hand had been chiseled off. A little notice pasted on to a piece of plywood stated that this was the final resting place of Sir Richard Mauncey. The damage to his effigy had been caused by soldiers during the English Civil War.

Back at the church door, Tim noticed a table bearing a pile of booklets giving the history of the church. They were fifty pence each. He felt in his pocket, dropped his money into the collection box, opened a copy of the pamphlet and started to read. On the fifth line down, it hit him.

"Bingo!"

He hurried out of the church to discover Pip standing in the graveyard, halfway along the north wall of the building.

"You were right!" he called, waving the pamphlet. "Guess what I've found!"

"Me first," Pip said, as he reached her.

She pointed to a low gravestone made of a slab of flint and leaning at an angle, from which she had rubbed the lichen. Upon it were inscribed the words: *Thomas Rawne Esq. of Rawne Barton. Dec'd the 12th day of May Anno Domini 1440 — Requiescat in pace.*

"Sebastian's father," Tim remarked quietly. Then he opened the flimsy guide. "Now listen to this." He began to read. " *'The parish church of Brampton is dedicated to two saints. Saint Benedict, the founder of western monasticism, was the saint who established the Benedictine Rule. At one time, there were over forty thousand monasteries practising his doctrine, the monks calling themselves Benedictines. The famous monastery at Monte Cassino in Italy, much damaged in World War II but now restored, was founded by him. He is the patron saint of farmers and . . .'* " Tim paused for effect, " *'. . . of those fighting or harmed by witchcraft.'* And that's not all. Get a load of this. *'The Blessed Raymond Lull, also known as Doctor Illuminatus, was the first Christian missionary to Islam in the thirteenth century. He was considered to be an alchemist who invented his own Christian interpretations of the alchemical mysteries, and is said to have succeeded in turning lead into gold, using this to finance his missionary work. A small number of his followers, known as Lullists, secretly continued his work after his death.'* "

He closed the guide and folded it into his pocket.

"Seems like Brampton and the countryside around has been a hotbed of jiggery-pokery for centuries."

"And still is," Pip added.

Leaving the churchyard, they returned to the main street and set off along the line of stalls, jostling their way through the crowd of shoppers. On the other side of the road, they caught a glimpse of their mother standing at a stall selling fresh meat.

"Ten pence says it's chops," Tim said.

"Sausages," Pip rejoined, "and you're on."

At the end of the street was a stall, smaller than the rest, selling secondhand books. Tim stopped in front of the cloth-covered table and began to look at the titles. Towards the front were used paperbacks, tatty copies of bestsellers with lurid covers, or older hardbacks missing their dust jackets. According to which row they were in, each book cost either one or two pounds. Behind them, on a rack of shelves, were larger editions, travel books on Asia, novels in better condition than those below, biographies and assorted nonfiction. On the topmost shelf were several dozen leather-bound books, their bindings cracked and the gold-leaf lettering on their spines faded.

Tim ran his eye along them, studying the titles — *The Gentleman's Magazine: 1805, Paley's Natural Theology, The Poetical Works of Lord Hervey* and *Boswell's Life of Johnson* in six volumes. It was not until he was halfway along the shelf that a slim volume took his attention. It was bound in red morocco leather with gold tooling and was entitled *The Ordinall of Alchimy.*

"Pip," Tim called out.

His sister, who was two stalls away looking at arrangements of dried flowers, scented candles and bottles of aromatic oils to add to potpourri, came over to the bookstall.

"What is it?" she asked.

"Look at this," Tim said, and he reached for the book.

An old man appeared from behind the shelves. He wore a grubby checked cloth cap, an old jersey with two buttons missing, a shirt without a collar and baggy corduroy trousers.

"What d'you want?" he snapped.

"I'd like to see that book, please," Tim replied.

"Which one?"

The old man leaned forward, in front of Pip and Tim, to look at the shelves. He smelled foul — of rancid tobacco, sweat, stale beer, unwashed feet and moldy cloth. His face was slack-jowled, grime ingrained in the wrinkles, his eyes almost colorless, watery and weak.

"That one," Tim said. "The thin one in the middle, to the left of *Poems upon Several Occasions*."

"Norton's *Ordinall*," the old man sneered. "That's not for you."

"How much is it?" Tim inquired.

"More than you've got. And I've told you, it's not for you."

"I'd like to see it, please," Tim persisted, being as polite as he could.

"You can't," the old man replied tartly.

"I only want to see it," Tim said, somewhat belligerently.

"This isn't a library," the old man retorted. "Go away."

"You can't sell many books if you don't let people look at them," Tim observed.

At this, the old man raised his hand. The fingers were bony, the knuckles arthritic, the nails thick and long and the color of horn.

"Begone, boy," he muttered threateningly, "or I'll rip your bloody ears off."

Tim and Pip stepped backwards. All around them, shoppers came and went, women carrying baskets or pushing baby buggies, two men carting a heavy armchair between them, another lifting a cardboard box full of old postcards into the back of a van.

The old man took two steps out from his stall, making as if to reach out at Tim. But then, as if having second thoughts or considering the boy was not worth the effort, he lowered his arm, turned and disappeared behind the bookshelves once more.

"Close shave!" Tim exclaimed. "Weird old coot."

"Talk about BO!" Pip said, wrinkling her nose. "He smelled like a farmyard."

"Let's put it this way," Tim replied. "I don't think he's shaken hands with Mr. Soap recently."

When Pip and Tim got back from the town, Sebastian was waiting for them. Mrs. Ledger invited him in and they sat down at the kitchen table to a lunch of sausages and mashed potato. Tim, having lost the bet, paid his sister ten pence.

Their mother's invitation, both Pip and Tim knew, was more than a pleasantry. Mrs. Ledger wanted the opportunity to quiz Sebastian further about his past. However, by good chance, a representative from the developers who had restored the house arrived to sign off the property just as they sat down to eat. This meant Mrs. Ledger had to leave the kitchen and go around the entire building with him while he inspected it and she pointed out minor defects to him that needed attention.

"Sebastian," Pip said, once her mother had left the room, "Tim and I went into the churchyard in Brampton today. We found your father's grave."

"It is to the north side," Sebastian replied.

"Do you . . ." Tim was not quite sure how to phrase it, ". . . go to see it at all?"

"I need not," Sebastian said. "The grave is but a monument to him. It means nothing to me, for it is empty."

"Empty!" Pip and Tim repeated in chorus.

"Of course. My father was burned at the stake. There was nothing of him to bury."

"But . . . what about his ashes?" Tim said.

"They were scattered by the wind, absorbed into the soil. I like to think," he went on, "that my father lives still in the flowers of the field."

To this, neither Pip nor Tim could think of a response. It seemed to them utterly bizarre that a relative could be, for all intents and purposes, buried in the garden.

"If your father was an alchemist," Pip asked at length, "why was he was given a monument in a Christian cemetery?"

"My father was, as am I, a Christian."

"But," Tim continued his sister's train of thought, "how could he be a Christian and yet still be an alchemist? Surely, if you were an alchemist, then you were involved with magic and that was . . ."

"Heretical?" Sebastian suggested.

"Yes," Tim said.

"It is recorded," Sebastian said, "that the great Saint Dunstan carried out alchemical experiments and, one day, had Satan himself appear before him, whom he caught with a pair of tongs from the fire and held by the nose as he screamed and howled. What you must understand," he went on, "is that there were Christian alchemists as well as those who were heretics or atheists."

"Like Blessed Raymond Lull?" Pip suggested.

Sebastian laughed quietly and said, "You have been much engaged in study."

"Not really," Tim admitted, and he pulled the church guide out of his pocket.

Sebastian put down his knife and fork, then, reading the introduction to the guide, announced, "It is time for you to know more. My father was one of those whom they called Lullists. This is why he was so feared by his enemies, for they were sorely afraid that, being a Christian, he might call down the wrath of God upon them. You will recall his patron, Henry Beaufort, was a cardinal and Bishop of Winchester, who would not have associated with a practitioner of the black arts. Humphrey, Duke of Gloucester, had no such principles, hence his alliance with Pierre de Loudéac."

"What does *Doctor Illuminatus* mean?" Pip inquired.

"*Illuminatus* means *he who enlightens*," Sebastian translated. "After Blessed Raymond's death, whoever became the leader of the Lullists took upon himself that appellation. My father was known thus."

"Your father was head of the Lullists?" Tim ventured.

"Indeed. Blessed Raymond died in the year of Our Lord, 1315. He is buried in the church of Saint Francis in Palma, upon the island of Majorca. My father was the fifth to be so named. Yet, by the time my father passed into heaven, there were but few Lullists remaining. Most had drifted from the Christian way, corrupted by the aspirations of the dark side of alchemy, which science they used for their own ends."

"And now?"

"The night before they put him to his death, my father passed to me this honor, for he said I was no longer an apprentice. I am, therefore, Doctor Illuminatus in my father's place."

For a long moment, Pip and Tim were silent. It seemed incredible that this boy, sitting at their kitchen table, was not only nearly six hundred years old and an alchemist, but the only survivor — indeed, the leader — of a secret religious sect dating back to the thirteenth century.

"This is hard, as you put it, for you to get your head 'round," Sebastian said.

Tim laughed and, collecting up the dirty plates, replied, "Now you're talkin'!"

As he slid the cutlery and plates into the racks of the dishwasher, Pip said, "Tim, tell Sebastian about the book."

"The book?" Sebastian repeated.

"Yes," Tim began. "When we were in Brampton this morning, the market was on. I found a second-hand bookstall. Most of the stuff was junk, but there were some old books on a shelf. One of them was called *The Ordinall of Alchimy*."

"You saw this?" Sebastian asked, almost incredulously.

"Right there on the shelf. You know about it?"

"*The Ordinall of Alchimy* was written in the year of Our Lord 1477, the author an alchemist called Thomas Norton of Bristol. Did you open it?"

"I wanted to look at it, but the old man running the stall refused. Smelly old bloke!"

Tim closed the dishwasher door.

"What did you say?" Sebastian said.

"I wanted to, but the book —"

"No, not the book. The man. You said he smelled."

"Like a tandoori fart," Tim chuckled.

Sebastian stood up, immediately agitated.

"This was no old man. This was de Loudéac."

Pip felt her spine crawl, just as it had done that first night in Rawne Barton when she discovered the bats flying out of the eaves of the roof. It occurred to her now that perhaps they had not been bats at all, but de Loudéac's minions reconnoitering the place, or leaving it, driven out by the arrival of her and her family after a decade of living there unmolested.

"How do you know?" Tim said. "He was just an old bloke selling some crappy books, who needed a bath."

"He is known also by another name. Malodor."

"Malodor?" Pip echoed.

"They called him this in Gloucester's household," Sebastian explained. "Malodor. It is from the French *mal odeur*. A bad smell. The smell of evil."

"So he shape-shifted into an old man?" Tim asked.

"No," Sebastian answered quietly. "What you saw was him."

It was now Tim's turn to feel edgy. He had stood right next to de Loudéac, talked to him and, worse, talked back to him.

"I shall go to the town immediately," Sebastian announced, "to see if I might locate him, but shall return before nightfall. Please thank your mother for my repast."

"Do you want me to come with you?" Tim offered. "I know where the stall is and what he looks like."

"No," Sebastian answered bluntly. "This I shall do."
And with that, he was gone.

By early that afternoon, the river level had dropped.
After the rain, the trout would be feeding well, for the
warm sunlight would be bringing out a fresh hatch of
mayflies. Tim picked up his fly rod and walked across
the meadow to the river.

Determining not to go upstream from the Garden of
Eden, he chose a section of deep water and began to
cast out into it. As he often did when he went fishing,
he worked the water thoroughly, casting in a pattern
until he found where the fish were, but his mind was
on other things.

His meeting with de Loudéac had unnerved him. It
was one thing for Pip to be chased by insects, but quite
another for him, albeit unwittingly, to be in the close
proximity of a man who, by all accounts, was in league
with Satan himself. He could not get rid of the image of
the scrawny, gnarled hand raised as if to strike him, could
not forget those words — *I'll rip your bloody ears off.*

No adult had ever spoken to him like that, threat-
ened him like that. It had been as if, for a few moments,
the rules by which civilized people lived had been dis-
carded, and it scared him. His world, Tim thought, was
so safe, so ordered. He was, he realized, lucky to live in
a comfortable home, to be the child of loving parents.
Now, this man — this creature — had entered into that
world and put it in jeopardy. Worse, there was nothing
he could do except trust to luck. And Sebastian.

It was, Tim considered, incredible how a boy of his own age could come to terms and battle with such malevolence. Admittedly, Sebastian possessed his father's knowledge, not to mention a bag of tricks that any television magician would have drawn his own molars out with a monkey wrench to attain, yet it still remained that he put himself at risk just for a principle, just for the sake of fighting evil.

His reverie was broken by a shout.

"Hey! Lad!"

Tim looked up. Coming along the bank towards him, from the direction of the Garden of Eden, was a middle-aged man wearing green wellington boots, a waxed waistcoat over a checked shirt and a cloth cap into the brim of which were stuck a number of gaudy trout and salmon flies. He was carrying a long walking stick like a shepherd's crook, with a hook made of a deer's antler at the top.

"Who are you, son?"

"Tim Ledger," Tim replied, reeling his line in.

"Do you have permission to fish here?" the man asked.

"Yes," Tim replied. "My father owns this field and the next, up as far as the fallen bridge. We've just moved into Rawne Barton."

"So you're the new family. That's all right, then," the man responded. "I'm the water bailiff for the Cromer Arms, the pub on the road to Stockwold. They own the fishing rights on both banks as far as your stretch. Their beat ends at the ruined bridge. This time of year, we have to keep an eye out for poachers. The days are long and the salmon are on the run." He grinned in a friendly fashion. "Do you have your Water Board fishing license?"

"I think so," Tim said, and he lowered his rod and landing net to the grass. Reaching into his pocket, he took out the small aluminium tin in which he kept his flies. He had put his license under the foam padding for safekeeping. Opening the lid, he removed it. "Here it is."

As he reached out to hand over the sheet of folded paper, the breeze shifted. For the briefest of moments, Tim caught the slightest whiff of a farmyard — rotting straw, cow dung.

"Thank you, son," said the bailiff, hooking his walking stick over his arm, taking the license and unfolding it.

Tim put the fly box back in his pocket, bent down and picked up his rod and net. He waited until the man was reading the license and then, taking a deep breath, spun round and took to his heels as fast as he could go. He seemed to be leaping over the field, his steps gargantuan, spurred on and made large by his fear.

"Oi! You!" a voice shouted from behind him.

Yet Tim did not care. He sped on. If the bailiff had a problem, he could come to the house and sort it out with his father. This was his land, he did own the fishing rights and the license was up to date. He had not broken the law.

Something appeared over his shoulder. Tim caught sight of it out of the corner of his eye. It was the crook on the top of the walking stick, angled to snare him by the neck. He ducked and kept going, his body almost falling forward under the momentum of his running.

It was then it hit him. First, the air around him went

liquid as if a bomb blast were running through it. This was followed by a hot, nauseous wind that scorched the nape of his neck as if, quite suddenly, he were being sunburned. A second later, he was struck by a sound such as he had never heard: neither a shout nor a scream, neither a yell nor a bellow. It was all of these rolled into one. And more. It filled his head, searing it through with the most terrible pain. It was like having toothache in his brain. Tim dropped his fishing tackle and instinctively put his hands to his ears. In vain. The sound seemed to be rising through him, as if from the ground, running in shock waves along his arteries, curdling his blood. He could not breathe.

His flight was reduced to a stagger. He was not sure now in which direction he was going. He opened his eyes to get his bearings. Ahead of him, across the field, was the river. To his alarm, he realized he was now heading towards it.

Standing on the bank was the bailiff. He was now at least four meters tall, almost the height of the riverside willows. The walking stick had grown as well. It was three meters long, the hook as big as that of a dockside crane. The bailiff's legs were astride, his hands on his hips, his arms akimbo and his head thrust forward. Wide open, his mouth was a round black hole in the bottom of his face which was puce, his eyes staring, his brow furrowed with effort. Tim could see his lips rimming yellowed fangs.

Gradually, as he watched it, the mouth closed and the volume of the sound lowered. As it did so, the bailiff grew smaller. Finally, the sound was gone — and the bailiff too.

His head ringing, Tim collected his fishing tackle and stumbled towards the house. What he wanted most of all now was a full dose of aspirin. Yet, by the time he reached the ha-ha, his head was clear once more.

⁜

"He has the shout," Sebastian announced, when Tim finished recounting his experience.

"What shout?" Pip asked.

"There are men," Sebastian explained, "who have learnt the shout. Have you ever heard the story of Joshua?"

"Sure!" Tim said. "He brought down the walls of Jericho with his trumpet. It's in the Bible. But what's that got to do with a shout?"

"Sound vibrates," Pip declared. "We did it in science. If you get the vibrations just right you can agitate the atoms of something so much that it breaks up."

"I remember," Tim replied. "Like that ultrasonic gizmo the dentist uses to get the plaque off your teeth. But descaling a set of incisors is a far cry from knocking down the walls of a Middle Eastern city by blowing a bugle."

"It is only a matter of scale, Tim," Sebastian said. "It is thought that Joshua brought down the walls of Jericho not by literally blowing his horn, but by using this to command his army to march in step round the city. The pounding of their feet in unison set up vibrations that loosened the mud bricks of the ramparts, which collapsed. It was told that Hector, the Trojan, had the shout and that the warriors of Ireland drove back their

Viking enemies by screaming at them. De Loudéac has this power. And it is terrible, for his is a devil shout. If you had stood close, it would have killed you."

Tim felt the blood drain from his face. He had been scared stiff of the bailiff-that-wasn't, yet he had not considered that the man had been out to actually kill him.

"Now he's going after both of us," Pip said glumly.

"He attacked Tim to scare him off," Sebastian stated, "yet I am more concerned with why he has been attacking you, Pip. I feel you may have something he desires."

It was Pip's turn to blanch.

"What do you mean?"

"In Tim's case," Sebastian said, "de Loudéac drove him away. With you, he has taken something — a strand of your hair."

"And a drop of your blood," Tim added.

"What?" Sebastian snapped.

"It was the day we moved in," Pip recounted. "I was stung by what I was sure was a butterfly."

"But butterflies don't bite," Tim interjected.

"Indeed not," Sebastian agreed. "Describe it to me."

"Sort of browny and uninteresting," Pip recalled.

"With a yellow spot?" Sebastian asked.

"Yes," Pip said, terrified. She felt like someone being told they had contracted a terrible disease. She wanted to make light of the news, perhaps prove it wrong. "It did suck my blood," she admitted, "but only a tiny amount, for just a second."

"This is most serious," Sebastian replied. "De Loudéac is using you."

"Using me?" Pip could not stop her voice wavering with sudden fear. "For what?"

Sebastian ignored her question and said, "De Loudéac believes we are getting closer to him. Tell me, Tim, exactly where did he shout at you?"

"On the riverbank, maybe a hundred meters downstream from the Garden of Eden."

"From which direction did he come?"

Tim thought for a moment and answered, "He came from upstream. He said the pub's fishing ended where there used to be a bridge."

Sebastian considered these facts for a moment, then said, "He must be in the immediate vicinity."

"If that's so," Tim said, "we'd better warn the Moonbeamers."

"The Moonbeamers?" Sebastian repeated.

"The hippies. They call themselves the Moonbeamers. There's half a dozen of them living in the quarry."

"What sort of people are these?" Sebastian asked.

"Drop-outs," Tim said. "Dope-heads. Travelers."

"They're sort of gypsies," Pip intervened. "I suppose in your day they were like tinkers."

"I know of hippies," Sebastian said. "I mean, are they good people or are they bad?"

"They smoke pot and do their own thing," Tim went on, "live an alternative lifestyle. The crappy old vehicles they drive usually don't have a registration or an inspection. But I don't suppose they're bad. Not really, like, evil."

"Then we must indeed go there," Sebastian said urgently, "and warn them. They are in great danger."

"Was there a quarry here when your father was

alive?" Tim asked as they hurried across the meadow, passing the Garden of Eden.

"Yes, yet it was but small. I have heard told that it was started by the Romans who used the stone to build several villas hereabouts. In my father's day, stone was cut there for the building of houses in Brampton. Later, in the reign of Mad King George, much more stone was taken, hence the quarry's size today."

"And the bridge?" Pip asked.

"That was also made of stone from the quarry. It was built some time before my father came, for it was here when Rawne Barton was built. It was used to bring stone for the house. My father was permitted to charge a toll to those crossing it."

Tim stopped dead in his tracks.

"Look!" He pointed ahead. "The hippies must've got their act together."

Between the old stone piers of the bridge, two long thick planks of wood spanned the river, bound together in the center by a length of blue plastic rope.

"Really helpful of them," Pip remarked sarcastically, "giving the bailiff — de Loudéac — a way over the river like that." She looked across the makeshift bridge. "It's at least ten meters over to the other bank and," she added, her voice betraying more than a hint of reluctance, "five meters above the water. There's no way I can go over those planks. I don't like heights and they're no wider than a book."

"Our passage will be quite safe," Sebastian assured her, and, grinning mischievously, he took their hands.

Pip and Tim felt slightly light-headed, then found

themselves on the top of the stone pier on the opposite bank. Behind them, the plank was undulating slightly.

"Have we just walked over that?" Pip asked disbelievingly.

"All you need to have is control of your mind," Sebastian said bluntly. "Or," he added with a smirk, "pass that control to another."

They took the path up through the trees where Tim had followed Splice. Just before reaching the clearing beneath the old quarry face, Sebastian halted and closed his eyes.

"There has been much evil in this place," he whispered. "We must beware. Stay close to me. Be alert."

With that, they stepped into the clearing.

The two vehicles were where Tim had last seen them. The windows of the bus had the curtains drawn. The coachwork was decorated with a skillfully painted picture of the moon with a beam of light arcing out from it. There were silhouettes sitting upon it and waving. On the rear luggage compartment door was written *Moonbeamers Inc.* in psychedelic lettering. The van was unadorned. One of its tires was only half inflated.

Sebastian walked quickly to the campfire and, going down on his haunches, held his hand over the ashes. On the ring of stones forming a hearth was balanced a smoke-blackened pot, which he touched lightly.

"The ashes are still warm," he said, rising to his feet, "yet the water in the pot has cooled. It is at least two hours since this fire was last burning bright. How many do you say were living here?"

"I saw four men, two women and a baby," Tim replied. "And a dog."

Going over to the van, Sebastian studied it for a moment, then beckoned to Tim and Pip.

"See this," he said.

A section of the metal side panel looked as if it were rumpled.

"It's a dent," Tim decided, looking along the side of the vehicle and adding, "One of many. Looks like Splice hasn't passed his test."

"This is not a dent," Sebastian declared. "Run your hand over it."

Tim did so. The ridges in the metal were rounded, the paint smooth as if it had only just been sprayed on and then highly polished.

"Maybe he's repaired it," Tim ventured.

"No," Sebastian said, "This metal has been melted and then hardened again."

"Why would he do that?"

"This was not done by the hippy," Sebastian continued. "This was de Loudéac's shout. At close range, it can heat up metal so as to make it liquid."

"He's been here?" Pip murmured.

"Yes. And within the last few hours, probably after meeting Tim, whilst returning whence he came."

"If he went upstream," Tim reasoned, "then he was heading in the direction of Brampton. Do you think that is where he is staying?"

"I think it highly likely," Sebastian decided, "but he will not be conducting his magical working there. For that, he must be elsewhere, where there are no people who may observe him."

"If he's been here," Pip said quietly, "what has happened to the hippies?"

"Pray God they are at the market," Sebastian answered and, walking over to the bus, he tried the door handle. It was locked.

"What's this?" Tim pondered aloud, peering at a mark in the earth by the bus door. Impressed into the soil was what appeared to be the hoof print of a deer, two parallel slots with a pointed front, sloping down into the dirt.

"It is, indeed, the mark of a cloven hoof, that of a goat," Sebastian said.

"I didn't see any goats when I was here selling my fish."

"No," Sebastian agreed, "you did not, for this is no ordinary goat but de Loudéac in his caprine manifestation."

"Like, what?" Tim exclaimed.

"*What was he doing, the great god Pan,*" Pip recited, "*Down in the reeds by the river, Spreading ruin and scattering ban, Splashing and paddling with hoofs of a goat.*"

"Like, what?" Tim said again.

"We learned it in speech and drama," Pip replied. "It's a poem about the Greek god Pan, who had goat's feet. Caprine means goat-like . . ."

"The god Pan could induce terrible fear in men," Sebastian interrupted, "driving them mad. The word *panic* comes from his name. When he died, it was said a great voice proclaimed his passing along the whole coast of ancient Greece."

"A great voice . . . ." Tim repeated.

"De Loudéac walks with the devil and has at his side the powers of chaos."

Pip touched Sebastian's arm.

"I can smell him," she whispered.

Sebastian, once again, held both their hands and said, softly, "We must begone from here."

Hand in hand, they set off down the path to the river. The odor grew stronger with each step. Pip held on to Sebastian as tightly as she could. She wanted to call for help but her terror prevented her. As Tim walked, he mentally counted off the landmarks he remembered.

Suddenly, he saw something beneath a bush. It was hairy, lying in wait for them. He thought he could see an eye, staring.

"Sebastian . . ." Tim muttered, looking straight at it, but Sebastian had already seen it.

They moved closer. The stink was now overpowering. The sunlight filtering through the trees flickered on something slick and wet and dark green, like the body of a snake.

Yet it was not a reptile. It was Woof, the hippies' mongrel. He was lying on his side, disemboweled. Behind him, deeper in the shadow of the bush, was something white. Tim moved the branches aside. Lying on the dried leaves and twigs was a severed human leg.

"Don't look, Pip!" Tim shouted, but it was too late.

"Oh, God! Oh, God!" Pip screamed.

Tim put his arm around his sister, averting her face. And as he did so, the leg and the corpse of Woof just dissolved into thin air.

# Six

# Artifice and Artistry

"Now you three behave yourselves," Mr. Ledger said, with a twinkle in his eye. "No helping yourselves to my cognac, no poker games, no dancing girls and no, I repeat no, circus performers."

"If we weren't new here," Mrs. Ledger added, somewhat frostily and clearly annoyed by her husband's flippancy, "you'd have a babysitter. As it is, we don't know anyone, so you're being left on trust."

"Come along, Barbara," her husband chivvied her. "They'll be all right."

"Thanks for letting Sebastian stay over," Tim said.

"Just so long as who needs to know knows," his father replied, holding his car keys up and jangling them in midair, at the same time giving his wife a brief but searching look as she fumbled in her handbag. "We're off. Be back about eleven."

"There are some sandwiches in the fridge," Mrs. Ledger announced, "and you can have the cheese, but not the gorgonzola. The Pepsis are in the cool-box compartment at the bottom of the door. Don't eat the cold chicken because that's for lunch tomorrow. And don't cook anything. There's a tub of Häagen-Dazs in the —"

"Barbara . . . !"

"Behave!" was her final, sternly delivered word.

The front door closed, promptly followed by the sound of tires on gravel.

Opening three cans of Pepsi, they went out and sat on deck chairs on the lawn, beneath the mulberry tree, overlooking the ha-ha and the meadow, with the river in the distance. Pip made quite sure she was not on the side nearest the Angel's Trumpet plant.

"What do you think happened to the hippies?" Pip ventured.

"One cannot speculate," Sebastian said matter-of-factly.

"Do you think they are all dead?"

"Perhaps," Sebastian said. "Perhaps not. It may be they are no longer in possession of their wits, that they are de Loudéac's now. If he has a use for them . . ." He left the rest unsaid.

They fell silent. The evening sun was low over the river and the fields and woods beyond it.

"It must be strange," Tim said, thinking out loud, "to live for so long, through so many centuries, and see how the world has changed."

"Evil never changes," Sebastian answered. "Only the means by which it seeks its end."

"You mean," Pip said, "you don't really look at how the world has altered? I mean, when you were a boy — or, rather, before you first hibernated — people must have just traveled by horse and cart. Now they have bicycles, cars, trains, aircraft." The more she thought about it, the more incredible it seemed. "Electric lights, telephones, wristwatches . . ."

"I have looked," Sebastian replied, "and I have learnt that which I need to know to assist me in my mission."

"So," Tim went on, "you know what cars are, but you don't know how they work and you can't drive."

"An automobile operates by the explosion of flammable liquids under pressure in a confined chamber, forcing down a piston which creates motion that may be disseminated through gears. This I know. Yet, in truth, the first car I came close to was that of your father, for my uncle owned no such vehicle."

"I think, sis," Tim announced, "it's time we educated Sebastian a bit, don't you?"

Taking Sebastian indoors, Tim switched on the television. This did not faze Sebastian: his uncle had had a television, albeit a black-and-white set. What did fascinate him, however, was the remote. He could not at first comprehend how the controls communicated with the television but, when Tim explained the principle of how it worked, Sebastian not only grasped the concept of infrared rays, but also pointed out that he understood the concept of black light which, he stated, was used by alchemists to create what he termed visual banishment. When Pip took Sebastian into the kitchen, he similarly understood the way in which the microwave worked, likening it to the heating effect de Loudéac's shout had had on the hippies' van. It was, he said, a matter of causing agitation in the atoms, which in turn created heat.

However, as the twilight deepened outside and they went upstairs, first locking all the doors and checking all the windows, Sebastian was to meet his match when confronted by Pip's CD player. The basic premise of what a laser was he could understand, but not how it read music from a silver disc and then played it.

"If you think that's cool," Tim said, "follow me. This'll blow your mind."

Tim sat Sebastian in front of his computer.

"Do you know what a computer does?"

"I assume it computes," Sebastian replied.

"Computes?"

"Conducts mathematical calculations," Sebastian responded.

"Well, in a way it does," Pip said. "Only in binary mathematics."

Sebastian looked puzzled. "Binary?"

"To the base of two," Tim explained. "But that's only the start of it. If you work to a base of only two, you have only two numerical possibilities. It's like having off and on. You can't have half off and half on. In the computer is a microchip. It is minute but, in simple terms, it contains millions of, like, little switches and these go on or off according to how an electric current flows through them and —"

"Just switch it on, Tim," Pip said.

The hard disk whirred, the cooling fan hummed and the monitor came on with the front-end graphics for Windows 2000. After a moment, the screen cleared to Tim's desktop.

"It is a television," Sebastian declared.

"No," Tim said, "it's a computer monitor. Watch this."

He leaned across in front of Sebastian, moved the

mouse up and clicked on *Start/Programs/Accessories/ Games/Solitaire*. He started the game but reached stalemate in ten moves with no more cards available to be played. He clicked on *Close* and returned to the desktop.

Sebastian stared at the screen for a moment. "How is this possible?"

"It's magic," Tim said, grinning. "But if you think that's something, watch this." He reached up to the rack on the bookcase beside his computer table. "A CD doesn't just have music on it."

Sliding open the CD-ROM drive, Tim put in *Mobil 1 Rally Championship*, turned up the volume on his subwoofer and plugged in his steering wheel to the spare USB port on the front of his computer. With a few keystrokes, he was ready to go. The roadside clock counted down and he was off, wheels spitting gravel, the engine screaming until he slipped up into second gear, then third. The stage he chose to drive was a short one, less than two miles: it took him eighty-three seconds.

"It is thus when driving a car?" Sebastian asked.

"Only rallying," Tim answered, sliding the steering wheel across the desk and pressing it down on its suckers. "Your turn. And after this, I'll fly you to Paris."

Pip left them to it and returned to her room, switching on her own computer, her father's last notebook computer. For her, a computer was not a glorified games console: it was a tool to help her with her studies, surf the Internet and create. Where her brother drove rally cars, flew airliners and played pinball, she painted and drew cartoons with the aid of a graphics pad, animating them with a program that her father had bought for his work as a television-commercial producer but no longer used — and composed music with a software package called *MusicWrite*. The latter was superb, for it allowed her to connect her keyboard to the sound card in the notebook so that what she played appeared as printed music on the TFT screen.

She glanced at the clock. It said 10:38.

After ten o'clock it was what her father termed a Ledger House Rule that no one played music or computer games except with earphones. This rule was suspended when her parents were out, but Pip still preferred to wear hers. They helped her to concentrate, all the more so now that the sounds of screaming car engines were coming from Tim's room.

Slipping the earphones over her head, she plugged them into the computer. Since the family had moved to Rawne Barton, she had not worked on her latest composition. Turning the volume up with the touch pad, she set the program running. It was a classical piece about ten minutes long, which Pip hoped she might have the school orchestra perform one day — that was, she now considered, if Bourne End Comprehensive had an orchestra. She had already laid down a track with the basic melody and was now adding more instruments to it.

As the music built to a climax, her head filled with sound. The oboe was rich, the clarinet fluid, rising through the notes to a point where, suddenly, the violins joined in. She admitted to herself, listening to it again, that it did bear more than a passing resemblance to Gershwin's *Rhapsody in Blue* but, as Mr. Bax, the music teacher at her last school, had told her, all art is imitative of itself. That was her excuse, anyway.

The music faded, the score moving across the screen as the instruments fell silent, one by one, to leave just the clarinet. That too, in turn, drifted away.

As the last note died out, Pip noticed a repetitive scratching noise. Puzzled, she clicked on *Media Player* and played just the last ten bars of her composition. When the last hint of music was gone, the interference remained although the green line of the wave signal was absolutely horizontal.

Pip removed her earphones. The noise persisted. Perhaps, she thought, it was some game Tim and Sebastian were playing. Yet the sound coming from Tim's room was now the low, insistent hum that one might hear in the cockpit of a Boeing 747-400 on autopilot. She turned to switch off the computer, catching a brief glimpse of her face reflected in her bedroom window.

But her face was superimposed over another's. Above it was a black top hat, hair hanging down on either side in dreadlocks that shone as if they had been oiled.

Pip opened her mouth and screamed.

The face did not move, but one of the eyes winked at her.

She became conscious of feet running in the passage outside her bedroom door. Tim and Sebastian rushed in.

"What's up, sis?" Tim asked.

Pip could do nothing but grab her brother's arm and point at the window, another scream filling her mouth yet somehow not able to escape.

Tim followed her finger and exclaimed, "It's Splice!"

He prized Pip's hand off his arm. Her fingers were stiff with fear. Sebastian took her hand.

Moving towards the window, Tim shouted, "Splice! What do you think you're doing? This is my sister's bedroom. You can't just . . ."

A hand appeared from below the window sill and, as if with extreme politeness, lifted the top hat. Splice's skull had been caved in, the soft pinkish sponge of his brain exposed, blood trickling down the dreadlocks.

The scream escaped from Pip's mouth, but it was not so much a piercing shriek as a squeak, such as a rabbit might make, trapped in a snare.

A bright light shone from somewhere in the distance. By it, Tim could see Splice was not alone. Hovering in the air behind him were the other hippies. Abby was just a disembodied head, the flesh of her neck hanging in ragged tatters. Reedy was grinning lewdly, his lips spattered with blood. Dark Horse held up the severed leg Tim had seen under the bush and was waving it as he might a club. Filomena, her hair disheveled like a grotesque halo around her face, held Starlight upside down by one leg, as a miscreant child might hold an unloved teddy bear.

The sound Pip had heard was that of Gazer grinding his teeth, which had been filed to points.

The light grew brighter and split into two beams, like brilliant halogen eyes in the darkness. They were rapidly approaching the house, moving fast across the field.

In an instant, the hippies were gone. The eyes moving towards the house were extinguished. All that was left was a small, nondescript moth scrabbling against the windowpane, attracted by Pip's bedside lamp.

From downstairs came the sound of a door slowly opening, footsteps and a voice which called out, as if reciting a nursery rhyme, "We're back! We're back! It's time to hit the sack. No time to take another tack. We're off to hit the sack."

Another voice said, "I hope you remembered not to touch the chicken."

"Did you sleep well?" Mrs. Ledger asked Sebastian at breakfast the following morning.

"Yes, thank you very much, Mrs. Ledger," Sebastian replied, casting Pip a sidelong glance. "It was much more comfortable than my normal bed."

"Would you like me to drive you home?" Mrs. Ledger offered. "I shall be going into Brampton with Pip. I have some shopping to do and Pip has a doctor's appointment later in the morning. I can easily drop you off."

"It is most kind of you, Mrs. Ledger," Sebastian said, "but I would not wish to inconvenience you."

"You don't have a bicycle," she came back. "It must be a long walk to your home. And I assure you, it will not inconvenience me one . . ."

"We're going fishing," Tim butted in, rescuing the situation and bringing an end to his mother's oblique inquisition.

Pip and her mother departed as soon as breakfast was over, leaving Tim and Sebastian in the kitchen. Together, they cleared away the breakfast plates and boxes of cereal.

"Why does de Loudéac keep on targeting the house?" Tim mused. "Is it you he's after?"

"I think not," Sebastian said. "He knows of me, of my whereabouts. It would be much easier for him to catch me off my guard away from the house, which is where he knows I have my greatest power. For de Loudéac to come here is, from his point of view, foolish."

"Is he trying to scare us out?"

"Again, I think not. We do not hide here. We frequently leave this sanctuary. He has plentiful opportunity."

"Is it, like," Tim considered, "he's sending in his troops to spy on us?"

"Once more, I think not. Why use his cohorts? He need dispatch but one mouse to be his spy. One ant. No," Sebastian said, "he wants something, yet I cannot assess what it is."

"How can we find out?"

"With ease," Sebastian replied, and he smiled. "This morning, I think we shall go a-hunting. Do you possess a bicycle?"

Ten minutes later, the house locked up and the alarm system activated, they set off for Brampton. Tim rode his mountain bike while Sebastian took Mr. Ledger's racing cycle. All down the drive and for the two hundred meters of road, Sebastian weaved from one side of the road to the other, much to Tim's dismay.

"You can ride a bike, can't you?" he asked Sebastian nervously, all the while listening out for any approaching vehicle.

"I have been known to," came the reply, "but it is not a mode of transportation with which I am familiar nor have any great experience."

By the time they had covered a mile, however, Sebastian was more steady and coped well even when a large truck overtook them.

"If we meet my mother in town . . ." Tim began as they freewheeled down a gentle slope in the road.

"You need not be worried on that account," Sebastian reassured him. "She will not see us."

They reached the town, and Sebastian pulled up outside a garage.

"We shall leave the bicycles here," he announced, dismounting and heading for a huge pile of old tires waiting to be taken away for disposal.

Tim was worried. "What if somebody finds the bikes and nicks them?"

"Nicks?"

"Steals, pilfers, filches, walks off with . . ."

"They will be quite secure," Sebastian said, disappearing round the corner of the tire mound.

Tim followed him, leaning his mountain bike against his father's racer.

"What next?" he asked.

"Our plan now is to seek out de Loudéac in the town. This will not be hard. I believe I will be able to locate him, for I have come to know his ways."

"And we can always follow our noses," Tim added wryly.

"In a manner of speaking," Sebastian replied. "In fact, we shall follow my nose." He stood with his feet apart, his hands on his hips. "And now for our disguise."

"Disguise!" Tim said. "What disguise?"

"It is time, Tim," Sebastian answered, "that you undertake the experience of shape-shifting."

At this, Sebastian put his hand on Tim's shoulder and murmured something in what Tim assumed was Latin. He felt slightly odd for a few seconds, but it passed.

Sebastian had vanished. Tim looked around, wondering what he should do next.

A Jack Russell terrier appeared from behind the tire stack. It was white with brown markings.

"If you contrive to call me Patch or Spot," the dog declared, "I shall be mortified. Try to think of something more original."

Tim's mouth fell open.

"Come, Tim," the dog continued. "You are to take me for a walk around the town. I shall direct us. You just follow. Now, attach the leash to my collar and we shall be on our way."

Although he had no idea how it had got there, Tim found he was holding a dog lead and did as he was told.

"It *is* you, isn't it?" Tim ventured. "I mean, like, you're Sebastian."

"Indeed," replied the Jack Russell. Its lips lifted in a canine smile.

"This," Tim said, "could be fun."

Sebastian the terrier tugged on the lead and they set off. Looking back to check the bicycles were safe, Tim could see no sign of them whatsoever.

They had not gone fifty meters along the pavement before, ahead of them, Pip and her mother stepped out of the baker's shop. Tim's step faltered. The terrier looked up.

"Don't be concerned. Walk on," the dog said, although the words sounded more like a canine snarl than a sentence.

"Where to next, Mum?" Tim heard his sister ask.

"The greengrocer's," his mother decided. "They sell bedding plants."

With that, they turned towards Tim and Sebastian the Jack Russell. Playing the part, the dog started wagging his tail furiously, tugging Tim in the direction of his mother and sister. He steeled himself for the encounter.

Sebastian uttered a little yelp of greeting.

"Hello," Pip said, bending to stroke him. Then, looking straight at Tim, she asked, "What's his name?"

What on Earth, Tim thought, was going on? Here he was, walking through Brampton with a dog on a lead and neither his sister nor — of all people — his mother saw fit to take him to task for it.

Flustered and nonplussed, he replied, "Patch." He was tempted to add *What's the matter with you two?* but resisted it.

The dog cast him an askance look, jumped up on his hind legs and gave Pip a quick lick on her chin.

"He's certainly a happy little chap," Tim's mother said. "Come along, Pip."

Pip gave the dog a final rub behind its ear and went off after her mother. It was then Tim caught sight of himself in the baker's shop window. He was a middle-aged, white-haired lady in a prim, two-piece suit and a white blouse with a rhinestone brooch shaped like a butterfly pinned to it.

"Patch!" the dog muttered with disdain.

"Never mind your name," Tim replied. "Do I really look like . . . like a retired primary-school headmistress?"

"If you think you look thus," Sebastian said, "then thus you look and thus will others see you. Now, let us continue our hunt."

"You could at least have made me into a man," Tim complained, but Sebastian was already at the end of his lead, tugging hard.

They reached the post office. Coming down the steps was a shabbily dressed old man walking with the aid of an adjustable cane, a scratched leather shopping bag in the other hand. For just a moment, Sebastian stiffened. He need not have bothered. Tim caught the unpleasant and now all-too-identifiable whiff of sweat, urine and cheesy feet.

The old man stood by the letter box, surveying the street, taking in every detail with his shifty eyes. To kill time and disguise their presence, Sebastian cocked his leg against a bus-stop sign.

Not believing himself to be not under observation, de Loudéac set off along the pavement. He walked with a shuffling gait, leaning on the stick, his back slightly hunched, but his head up, facing forward, looking hastily from side to side every dozen steps.

Tim and Sebastian followed at a distance, Tim pausing to look in a shop window every now and then, Sebastian sniffing at lampposts, a black-and-gold trash bin and a terra-cotta trough full of flowers outside Curlers 'n' Clippers, the ladies' hairdresser's salon.

They had to stop longer than usual by the flower display as de Loudéac was studying the headlines at a newsstand. Tim, concentrating on their quarry, did not notice the hairdresser glaring at him through the window, nor did he see the door open.

"Excuse me, madam," the hairdresser said.

Not realizing he was being addressed, Tim continued to watch de Loudéac surreptitiously.

"I said," the hairdresser repeated starchily, "excuse me, madam."

Tim turned, to be confronted by a woman in a pink pinafore, with an array of hair clips attached to the neck strap.

Sebastian started to lift his hind leg.

"I would be most grateful," the hairdresser continued tartly, "if you would take your dog elsewhere. Those flowers cost a lot of money."

Sebastian let out a tiny squirt of urine and lowered his leg.

"Well, really!" the hairdresser exclaimed with disgust. "Some people have no respect for the property of others."

"I'm terribly sorry," Tim apologized. "I'm afraid my mind was elsewhere. Patch! You naughty boy!"

The hairdresser turned on her heels in a huff. Tim coughed. Had that really been his voice? All fruity, upper-crust and plummy . . .

"You should control your dog better," whined the Jack Russell, and he tugged on the leash.

De Loudéac went a short way, then turned into the butcher's shop.

"Go in and see what he's buying," Sebastian growled.

Tim tied the lead to a hook in the butcher's shop wall, beneath a notice that read, *Please leave your dog here,* and went in. Sebastian sat and scratched behind his right ear with his right hind leg.

De Loudéac was standing at the counter, purchasing two lambs' hearts. When he turned to leave, he looked Tim straight in the eye.

"Good morning," Tim greeted him cheerily, glad the smell of the butcher's shop went some way towards disguising the old man's vile cocktail of body odors.

"It is for some," de Loudéac muttered, and he walked to the door where he stood, counting his change.

"What can I get for you, madam?" It was the butcher, wearing a white apron and a straw boater with a blue hatband.

Tim had to think fast. He had no money on him and he did not want to buy anything — yet to make no purchase, having entered the shop, would seem suspicious.

"Do you have any marrow bones?" he inquired. "For my dog," he added hastily.

"I'm sure we can find something for him," the butcher replied and, reaching into a tray under the counter, produced a huge bone. "Here we are. That'll keep him busy for a while. Shall I wrap it or," he looked over Tim's shoulder to where Sebastian was looking in from the door, not a meter from de Loudéac's feet, "would he like it straight away?"

"Straight away," said Tim, not wanting to be hampered by having to carry a bone down the street in a plastic bag.

De Loudéac had still not gone. Tim had to stall.

"How much is that?" he asked, ready to declare he

145

had forgotten his purse or left his handbag in the baker's, at home, in his car.

"No charge, madam," the butcher replied.

In a mirror behind the butcher, on which was engraved *B. Whitton & Son: Purveyors of Fine Meats & Poultry*, Tim was relieved to see de Loudéac step out into the street.

"Are you quite sure?" he asked, buying just a little more time.

"Quite," said the butcher with a smile. "I hope the little chap enjoys it." He laughed. "It's almost as big as he is."

Tim thanked the butcher and, taking the bone, went outside.

"There you are, Patch," he said loudly. "Here's a lovely big bone . . ." He lowered his voice. "And you can carry it. It'll teach you to drop me in it by swinging your leg on those flowers."

The Jack Russell did not say anything but gave Tim a filthy look, reluctantly took hold of the bone in his teeth and, once the lead was untied from the hook, set off after de Loudéac who was, by now, thirty meters away. At the first corner, he dropped the bone in the gutter.

De Loudéac's next stop was the fishmonger's stall Tim had seen on market day. He bought a piece of smoked haddock, placing it in his shopping bag with the lambs' hearts.

Tim bent down to pretend to adjust Sebastian's collar.

"What next?" he whispered.

"Now, I trust, we shall discover his place of domicile."

But de Loudéac did not head home. He went down a residential side street and stopped outside a house with a polished brass plaque by the door. There were no shop windows to linger at here. Tim and Sebastian had no alternative but to keep on walking, closer and closer to their prey. They were within five meters when de Loudéac took a few steps towards them and vanished down a cobbled passageway. Tim, not daring to follow him, stopped at the house door. The brass plaque read, *Keith Markham BVetMed., DVOphthal., MRCVS.*

"It's a vet's!" he exclaimed.

"Let me off the leash," Sebastian said urgently.

Tim undid the clip. The Jack Russell scampered off down the passageway. Seconds passed. Tim, unsure what to do, grew increasingly worried, glancing down the passageway, seeing nothing but the brick walls of the buildings on either side and a padlocked gate at the end. Then came the unmistakable, hysterical barking of a terrier.

Tim set off down the passageway, walking with as much speed as he thought a middle-aged woman might decently exhibit when looking for her dog.

At the gate, the passageway took a right-angled corner. Tim went round it to find Sebastian, no longer a Jack Russell, standing by a row of trash bins and green garbage bags printed *Incinerate only.*

"De Loudéac was in this place," he said, "but he dissolved before I got here."

"Where is he now?" Tim asked.

"I know not." Sebastian shrugged. "Yet tell me, what did he purchase in the butcher's shop?"

"Lambs' hearts. What was he doing here?"

Sebastian stepped aside.

"This," he said.

One of the green bags had been ripped open, its contents spilling out on to the cobbles of the passageway. Tim saw, spread about, the carcass of an old black Labrador-cross-collie dog with a gray muzzle, some offal that must have been the result of several veterinary operations and a dead cat. From its head, Tim could tell it had been a Siamese, yet that was the only clue to its identity. It had been flayed.

Sebastian's face held a grave look. "De Loudéac is collecting those pieces remaining that he needs to complete his homunculus," he said, "and I believe he must have nearly all he requires by now."

By the time Pip and her mother arrived at the doctor's office, just before noon, the waiting room was quiet. Most of the morning's patients had been seen, and all the doctors except Dr. Oliver had left to make house or hospital calls.

Pip was the third of three people to be seen by the doctor, who had set aside the last hour before lunch to carry out minor surgical operations. Ahead of her in line was a little girl of about five with a heavily bandaged arm and an elderly woman in a floral print dress.

A short while after the girl had been called into the

nurse's room by the doctor, the elderly lady, who was sitting opposite Pip and her mother, placed the copy of *Country Life* magazine she had been reading back on the magazine table and looked across the waiting room.

"Such a tiresome thing," she remarked, addressing Pip's mother. "A mole on my back. Very inconvenient." She briefly lowered her voice, adding conspiratorially, "It catches on my bra strap. Dr. Oliver says he'll freeze it off with liquid nitrogen. Science is such a wonderful thing."

"My daughter is having a wart removed by the same method," Mrs. Ledger replied. "I'm told it doesn't even cut the skin. It's like cauterizing with something very cold instead of very hot."

"And quite painless," the woman went on, smiling at Pip. "You'll not feel a thing. Where is your wart, dear?"

"On my thumb," Pip said, holding it up.

"Oh, that's just a little one," the woman declared. "Doctor'll have that off in a jiffy. But," she continued, "when I was a little girl, they didn't have liquid nitrogen. Do you know how we used to get rid of warts?" She did not wait for Pip's answer. "We had them charmed away. There was a man in the next village who could wish them away. You went to him and gave him a penny and then, a week later, your wart would be gone. Just like that! My mother used to say it was magic."

This talk of charms and magic put Pip instantly on the alert. If de Loudéac could be a blackbird, then transforming himself into a pleasant woman in a summer dress would be a piece of cake.

"There's no accounting for some things," Mrs.

149

Ledger commented. "Science is all very well, but there's a lot we don't know yet."

"Oh, you can be sure of that!" the woman responded. "Yes, indeed."

You can say that again, Pip thought.

The door of the waiting room opened, and the nurse poked her head round it to survey the room.

"Mrs. Polson?"

The elderly woman stood up. For not more than a few seconds, Pip could smell her perfume, an overpowering mixture of orange blossom, musk and patchouli oil. But behind it, like a bitter aftertaste, was the vague smell of putrid flesh.

The door closed after her.

"What a pleasant lady," Pip's mother remarked.

Pip was terrified. She was now certain the woman had been de Loudéac, shape-shifted into some country lady with a gift for small talk and a more than passing knowledge of witchcraft.

"You look as if you've seen a ghost," her mother said. "White as a cloud." She patted her daughter's hand. "Don't worry. It'll all be over in two shakes of a puppy-dog's tail. And it really won't hurt."

"No, Mum," Pip replied solemnly.

She could hardly tell her mother the truth, that the pleasant lady was a fifteenth-century alchemist who practiced the black arts and was in league with Satan and all his evil minions. Picking up a magazine, Pip tried to occupy her mind with the pictures of celebrities and their lives, but it was useless. De Loudéac was there, in the next room, having a mole removed from his back. And, she considered, wasn't a mole a sign of witchery? Then it dawned on her that so was a wart . . .

The door opened again and the woman came out.

"Nothing to worry about, my dear," she said as she passed Pip's chair. "All over in two shakes of a puppy-dog's tail."

Could she have heard her mother say that? Pip wondered. Had she perhaps, even from the next room, been eavesdropping on their conversation, gleaning any facts she might about Pip and her family? She watched as the woman left the waiting room, spoke briefly to the receptionist at the desk outside, then left the building.

"Philippa Ledger?" the nurse called from the door.

"Do you want me to come in with you?" Pip's mother asked.

"I'll be all right, Mum."

Pip stood and went into the nurse's room. It was as she had expected — a couch with a disposable paper sheet spread over it, several metal chairs, a metal desk with a white melamine surface, a stainless-steel trolley bearing several trays of surgical instruments half covered with a cloth and white cupboards on the wall. Hanging over the couch was a print of a farm scene while over the desk was a calendar advertising a drug company. The room was permeated with the overpowering smell of hospital disinfectant and medicines.

"Sit down here, please, Philippa," the nurse said, indicating a metal seat with an armrest attached to one side on a swivel. She studied a sheet of paper pinned to Pip's medical-record folder. "Just a wart to come off. This won't take long."

"Isn't Dr. Oliver going to do it?" Pip asked.

"No, the doctor was called away on an emergency. But that doesn't matter. This is a simple procedure and I can do it. Only the doctor can remove blemishes from the face. That's the law. But from a finger . . . that can be left to a lowly nurse like me."

She smiled and turned to the desk, picking up a gadget that looked not unlike Pip's father's gas-powered blowlamp.

"This canister," the nurse explained, "contains liquid nitrogen gas. It is very cold indeed. What I shall do is squirt tiny little bursts of the gas on to your wart. This instantly freezes it, and then I'll scrape it off with this . . ." she pointed to a steel instrument in a small steel dish ". . . spatula. This process is called cryosurgery."

Resting Pip's hand on the armrest, palm up, she swabbed the wart with surgical alcohol and, pulling over another chair, sat next to Pip and took hold of her wrist.

"All you'll feel is a cold sensation. Nothing to worry about. Ready?"

Pip gritted her teeth and nodded. The nurse put the nozzle to the wart and pressed a trigger. There was a brief fizzle. Pip felt nothing. This was repeated several times, then the nurse put aside the appliance and scraped the wart tissue off into the steel dish. Only at the end, when the base of the wart came out, did Pip wince.

"All done," said the nurse. "You may have a little blister form, but it's nothing to worry about."

"It's bleeding a bit," Pip observed.

"It will weep for a little while," the nurse reassured her, dabbing a gauze swab on the wound and applying a bandage. "If it does, just dab on a bit of antiseptic cream and a new bandage." She dropped the bloody swab in the dish with the scrapings of wart tissue. "Now, off you go."

Pip stood up and walked to the door.

"Thank you very much," she said, turning to the nurse as she reached the door.

Bending over the desk, the nurse was dropping the bloody swab and wart scrapings into an envelope. This she folded and placed in the pocket of her tunic.

"Aren't you supposed to throw . . . ." Pip began.

The nurse turned. Her face was contorted, her nose flat and wrinkled like a pig's, her eyes round and staring like those of a bird. Through her hair, one of her ears was pointed, the tip curling forward. Tufts of coarse, brindled bristles stuck out from it.

Panicking, Pip yanked on the door. It would not open. She wrenched the knob. The latch gave and she almost fell out into the waiting room.

"Was it that bad, darling?" her mother asked sympathetically, a worried look on her face.

Pip, firmly closing the door behind her and gathering her wits about her, replied, "No, Mum. I tripped on the step."

# Seven

# The Dead and the Undead

Two candles in bronze holders burned upon the table in the center of Sebastian's subterranean chamber. The flames glinted off the glass retorts and fractionating towers. On the shelves, the dark leather spines of his alchemical books shone like highly polished shoes.

"De Loudéac is ready," Sebastian announced.

"But why did he steal my wart?" Pip asked. "What possible use can he have for a bit of bandage with a drop of blood on it?"

"DNA," Sebastian answered. "Deoxyribonucleic acid, that which constitutes the genetic matter of all living things, the building blocks of life. If he has but a small amount, he can build upon it. As you would say, clone from it. He first had your blood from the stinging butterfly, then your cells from your hair, but these seem to have been insufficient."

"You mean," Pip said, horrified, "that the homunculus is *me*?"

"No, Pip," Sebastian assured her. "Not you, but it surely contains elements of you, something of your character that de Loudéac required."

"Such as?" Pip wanted to know and yet, at the same time, she did not.

"Perhaps your strength of character," Sebastian considered. "Perhaps your innocence, being, as you are in his eyes, a child. Perhaps your intelligence, which will complement another trait he has acquired elsewhere. For you see," he finished, "he is not making a replica of any one person. He is making a composite. A creature that is a fusion of human and animal characteristics."

"A lamb's heart, the Siamese cat's fur . . ."

"Precisely."

"But that's unnatural!" Pip retorted. "It's terrible."

"Indeed," Sebastian said, "it is against all the laws of Our Lord. Yet it is what he seeks to do, for he wants what he believes will be an invincible creature, one that contains the attributes of its many components."

"Brave as a lion, fast as a cheetah, quick as a snake," Tim commented.

Sebastian nodded.

"How can you be sure he is nearly ready?" Pip responded.

"I can be sure," Sebastian replied, "for tonight is a new moon and it is then that new life may be created."

He walked across the flagstones and, climbing the library steps, removed a small book from the top shelf. Pip and Tim moved to the table to read it over Sebastian's shoulder.

"This tome you may not see," Sebastian said, placing it on the table but not opening it. "Step back, I beg of you."

Somewhat offended, Pip and Tim retreated a few steps.

"We can be counted on not to tell a secret," Pip remarked in a pained voice.

"This I know," Sebastian said, "for I trust you. Yet this book contains matters not that I fear you will recount to others, but of which it is best you remain in ignorance, for your own good."

He turned the cover over and thumbed through a number of pages until he found what he was looking for. Slowly, his lips moving to the words, he ran his finger down the page. Tim could just see that it contained strange diagrams as well as text. When he was done, Sebastian returned the book to the shelf.

"De Loudéac," he said, "has to conduct a rite of conception in order to bring his homunculus fully to life. This cannot be accomplished in the town for it would draw much attention. He must find a place where he is safe from discovery, where he may channel and focus the powers of darkness."

"How does he do that?" Tim asked.

"He will use his surroundings," Sebastian explained, taking down another book and opening it at a copper-plate engraving of the interior of a church. "Consider this illustration. It shows the chancel of a twelfth-century church in Italy which, before the coming of Our Lord, Jesus Christ, was a pagan temple to the Greek god, Zeus. Notice how, behind the altar, the wall is curved, to form a semicircle. The roof above is domed. Imagine, if you can, that the walls and roof are hands, opened yet brought together as if to catch a ball. And imagine that the ball is the power you seek to bring to this place, in this case the power of the Almighty. The curve of the walls and the roof sweep this power inwards upon the altar —"

"It's like a satellite dish!" Tim exclaimed. "A concave shape that collects the signal and concentrates it in the middle where the receiving aerial is."

Sebastian opened an astronomical almanac.

"The moon rises at eleven forty-three of the clock. That is when he will be commencing his ritual." He looked across at Tim. "What is the hour now?"

Tim glanced at his watch and said, "Half past three. We've got eight hours to find de Loudéac's whereabouts."

"I think not." Sebastian produced a long leather tube from a rack beneath the table and, twisting off the lid, let a roll of pale vellum slide into his hand. "Draw near and see this."

He smoothed it out on the table, weighing down the corners with books. It was nearly a meter square.

"It's an old map," Pip declared.

Unlike a modern cartographer's map, it was as much a picture as a plan. Villages were shown as clusters of tiny houses, woods as hundreds of little trees. Marshy areas appeared covered in tufts of rushes or coarse grass, orchards as rows of trees with little red dots in them for fruit. Some fields contained primitive drawings of farm animals. On a trackway was the two-dimensional drawing of a man on horseback, not skillfully done, but as a child might, the horse's ears pricked up, its bridle painted blue, the man riding with his feet stuck out. Intricate symbols were inked in here and there, scattered seemingly willy-nilly about the landscape.

"More exactly," Sebastian corrected her, "it is an alchemical map of this area. This," he pointed to a little cluster of houses drawn in three dimensions, "is what is today Brampton. You can see here the mound upon which the castle stood. This," he ran his finger along two meandering lines, one drawn in faded azure ink, the other brown, "is the river and this is what is now the road from Brampton to Stockwold. As you can tell from the depiction of trees, this area was once covered with forest."

"It might be in color," Tim observed, "but it's certainly no Ordinance Survey map."

"What is this place?" Pip asked, her finger hovering over a carefully drawn cross with curled ends to the arms.

"Rawne Barton," Sebastian answered, "or, to be precise, it is the Roman spring in the field. This map was compiled before my father built the house. Do you see anything else that might be of interest?"

Side by side, Pip and Tim studied the map. It was Tim who finally spoke.

"Just here," he said, "across the river, there's a symbol drawn. Looks like an inverted horseshoe with something else in it. What does it mean?"

Unlike most of the other symbols, drawn in black ink, this was the color of dull brass.

Sebastian picked up a pencil and drew an inverted U upon a piece of paper, then, within it, added a symbol: ⊗

"Dismiss for the moment," he instructed them, "the U. This circle is an ancient sign dating back thousands of years before the time of Jesus Christ. It may be found on Bronze Age carved stones. To alchemists, it is the sign of phosphorus. Are you aware of this substance?"

"We learned about it in science," Pip announced. "It's really dangerous because it ignites spontaneously with air."

"It is the substance some alchemists called brimstone," Sebastian added, "that from which the fires of hell are created. Thus, on the map, where you see this symbol, be assured it is a place where the power of great evil may be concentrated."

"What about the upside-down U?" Tim asked.

"That," Sebastian said, "is not an alchemical sign."

"So what is it?"

"Study again the map, my friends."

Pip and Tim looked at the map once more, then at each other, then at Sebastian, and said in chorus, "The quarry!"

At ten o'clock, Pip told her parents she was tired and went up to her room. Ten minutes later, Tim said he thought he would turn in now too. Fifteen minutes after that, in the gathering summer dusk, they emerged from the coach house with Sebastian, wearing dark-colored clothes and soft-soled sneakers. Tim carried his father's black Maglite, a hefty halogen flashlight that took six batteries and was the size and weight of a policeman's club. Sebastian had armed himself with a small T-shaped piece of metal in which, at the point where the upright met the crossbar, was set a smooth, cloudy crystal.

"I suppose," Tim said as they set off through the long grass of the meadow, "that's a magic wand of some sort."

"In a manner of speaking," Sebastian replied. "I personally do not believe in the efficacy of wands. They are more the invention of writers of stories than genuine alchemical tools. This item has an actual practical use."

"What exactly is it, then?" Pip asked.

"It is an alchemical divining rod," Sebastian told her, "in the shape of the true cross. If I were to hold it by each end of the bar, the long section would bend upward if it encountered goodness, downward if wickedness."

"A bit like those birch sticks that dowsers use."

"Yes, save that their rods discover water and are made of wood, whilst this is made of gold."

"Gold!" Tim exclaimed. "Solid?"

"No, the center is of silver, but this is plated with gold."

"What about the stone set in it?" Pip said.

"It is of quartz," Sebastian replied. "It is called the eye of God for it sees righteousness and condemns wrong."

As they came near the river, they stopped talking. When they reached the bank downstream of the Garden of Eden, they turned and followed the river for about half a mile, leaving the grounds of Rawne Barton and making their way through the neighboring fields. Eventually, they reached a gravel track that crossed the river by a rusty iron girder bridge. Welded into the floor of the bridge were two rows of protruding bolts.

"This was a railway line," Sebastian explained, keeping his voice low. "It was closed many years since."

Once over the river, they found a track branching off from the former railway line, clearly a spur running towards the quarry. Some way along this, Sebastian stopped.

"From here," he said, "we shall climb to the top of the quarry. It is imperative we are silent. On such a still evening, sound will travel easily."

They entered a wood, the ground rising gradually at first, then, after a few hundred meters, more sharply. It was not easy going. They had to watch out for loose stones and dry twigs. When Tim stepped on one, it cracked like a pistol shot, drawing a scowl from both Pip and Sebastian. It took them half an hour of climbing to reach the top of the cliff.

The drop was greater than it looked from below, at least fifty meters. The rock face was broken in a few places by ledges but it was otherwise smooth. Lying on their stomachs, for safety as much as to keep hidden, they elbowed themselves forward until they could just see over the rim. The sky was clear and although the new moon had not yet risen there was sufficient starlight to see below.

In the clearing beneath the cliff were the hippies' bus and van. Where the Moonbeamers had had their hearth, another fire was burning, the thin smoke rising on drafts of hot air up the cliff face. It smelled sweetish, a delicate incense.

"Apple wood," Sebastian hissed. "To purify the air."

The door of the bus opened, a figure stepped out and the door swung shut behind it. Standing close to the vehicle, it gazed around itself before stepping towards the fire. As it approached the glimmer of the flames, Tim realized it was the old bookseller. He was wearing a black cape.

"De Loudéac!" Sebastian whispered.

Once more, the bus door opened and another figure appeared. It did not, however, follow de Loudéac to the fire but moved around the clearing, keeping to the shadows. Its movements were slow, hesitant.

"Is that . . ." Pip was not sure how to refer to the homunculus, ". . . it?"

"No," Sebastian answered. "That will not move until de Loudéac instills the force of life within it. What you see," he added, "is either Beelzebub or one of his infernal servants."

"Beelzebub?" Tim repeated.

"The Lord of Darkness," Sebastian murmured. "He whom they call Satan."

De Loudéac threw something into the fire. There was a sharp flash of brilliant light from the fire that momentarily illuminated the trees.

"Magnesium powder," Sebastian said. "It is beginning, we must move."

As cautiously, yet as quickly, as they could, Pip and Tim followed Sebastian down the side of the quarry, keeping just a few meters back from the edge of the drop and well within the cover of the trees. It took them less than ten minutes to reach the quarry floor, where they crouched behind some huge boulders.

By the fire, de Loudéac was chanting in a low, sonorous voice. On the periphery of the light of the flames, the shadowy figure danced a contorted jig.

Across the far side of the blaze, the old Royal Mail van stood with its back doors open. It was empty.

"What do we do now?" Pip whispered.

"I must position myself between the fire and the omnibus," Sebastian replied.

"Why?" Tim muttered. "That's crazy. There's no way —"

"I must," Sebastian reiterated. "If I can get the light of the fire to shine on the vehicle through the quartz lens . . ." He held up the T.

"What's with the bus?"

"The smaller vehicle is empty. Therefore," Sebastian reasoned, "within the omnibus must be de Loudéac's homunculus."

De Loudéac's chanting ceased. There was another flash of radiant light. The chanting started again, its rhythm more urgent.

Lying down and placing his head at ground level, Tim peered around one side of the boulder, Sebastian the other. The shadowy figure twirled in a tottering pirouette and entered the van. Immediately, the interior seemed to fill with dense black smoke. It closed the doors behind itself.

The chanting rose in volume.

"Now is our opportunity," Sebastian said in a low voice, just audible over de Loudéac's alchemical litany. "Pip, on my signal, I want you to walk out from behind this boulder. Take no more than a few steps. Just make yourself visible and call to de Loudéac." He thought for a moment. "Address him as Malodor. If he hears you not the first time, repeat this name until you have his attention, then fall silent. Make no other sound. Do not approach the fire. If de Loudéac should come towards you, step back and lower yourself once more behind the boulder. He will not come right up to you, for he dare not leave the glow of the fire. To do so will spell the failure of his endeavor. If he quits the fire, he cannot complete the ritual. Can you do this?"

Pip nodded. She was terrified at the thought of giving away her presence, but she knew she had no alternative. They had to stop de Loudéac.

"Tim," Sebastian ordered, "on my signal, you run towards the right-hand side of the fire, as fast as you may go. Stop where the path to the river begins. Make as much noise as you can. Wave your arms. Switch on your light. Flash it in de Loudéac's face. If he comes for you, show no fear. Stand your ground. He can do nothing to you except try to fright you. Be firm, hold to your resolve."

The chanting grew quieter and was now more melodious, like someone singing a psalm at the far end of a vast cathedral.

"What is your signal?" Pip whispered.

"When you see me, you will know," Sebastian answered. "Be ready!"

With that, Sebastian crept away, moving furtively from boulder to boulder in the direction of the bus.

Pip and Tim waited. Pip took her brother's hand and squeezed it.

"We'll be all right," Tim whispered. "We can trust him. I think . . ."

From the direction of the quarry cliff came a deep

yellow light. It seemed to be moving, shimmering and swaying. It was as if someone were approaching, carrying a bright lantern.

The chanting ceased. De Loudéac turned, raising his arms, his fingers outspread like clutching talons.

As the yellow light grew stronger, they could hear a voice. It was Sebastian's.

"I command you, Unclean One," he intoned, his words echoing off the quarry face, "along with all your minions, begone from this place."

De Loudéac picked up a log from the fire, holding it over his head like a firebrand. Tim could see he was holding it where it was alight, the skin of his fingers singeing. He seemed impervious to the pain.

"I command you to obey me to the letter. Depart hence, Transgressor. Depart, Seducer, full of lies. Give way, Abominable Monster, to Christ, Our Lord in Heaven . . ."

From beyond the bus, Sebastian appeared. The golden T glowed luminous in his hands. He glanced towards the boulder and nodded briefly.

"Now!" said Tim.

He jumped up and ran forward, yelling at the top of his voice, waving his arms. When he reached the path, he halted and switched on the flashlight. The beam cut through the faint smoke rising from the fire and illuminated de Loudéac's face. It was scarlet, his eyes pale green, like a cat's. Stepping to one side of the fire, he hurled the burning log at Tim. Tim watched as it arced through the air, spinning over and over on itself. It hit the ground to his left in a scatter of sparks.

"Malodor! Malodor!"

Tim looked over to the boulder where they had been hiding. Pip was standing before it, her hands clasped demurely in front of her.

De Loudéac started towards her, walking slowly, carefully. He might have been a hunter stalking his prey.

In an attempt to distract him, Tim shouted louder, wiggling the beam of light over de Loudéac's back. The alchemist ignored him.

Pip stood firm. Tim could almost see her legs quaking.

Sebastian edged forward. He was nearly at the fire now.

The doors of the van swung open. The cloud of black smoke wafted out, the air filling with the sound of a million angry bees.

"Look out!" Tim hollered.

Sebastian ignored the approaching cloud. He knelt and held the T close to the flames. The firelight danced on the quartz crystal. Tim saw a pinprick of light settle on the side of the bus. It was, he thought in a detached way, like the point of light he got using a magnifying glass to focus sunlight on a piece of wood to scorch his name on it.

There was nothing else to do. Despite all Sebastian had told him, Tim ran for the fire. He had no idea how he was going to stop the cloud from reaching Sebastian, but that was no matter. He had to do something.

Holding the T steady, Sebastian concentrated hard on the bus, keeping the beam of firelight as still as he could.

Two meters from the fire, Tim happened to look in

Pip's direction. De Loudéac had stopped some paces in front of her. She was resolute, but Tim could see by the firelight that her eyes were shut tight. As he watched, de Loudéac threw back his head, his eyes staring and his mouth opening wide.

"Pip!" Tim screamed. "Step back behind the boulder!"

Ahead of him, Sebastian began to speak slowly, carefully enunciating every word.

*"In nomine Dei, eo, eo, eo . . ."*

Now, de Loudéac's mouth was perfectly round. His shoulders rose slowly, his cloak spreading as he put his arms akimbo. Tim knew he was drawing in his breath.

"Pip! Run!"

De Loudéac thrust his head forward.

Tim was enveloped by the black cloud. Within it, the noise of the bees was deafening — yet it was not composed of bees. All around him swirled tiny devilish creatures. Their grotesque faces, covered with warts or layers of skin like the wattles of a turkey or the jaws of an old bulldog, dripping with spittle, seemed to mock him. Many were laughing at him, pointing at him, jeering and sneering.

There was a sudden, dazzling flash of light. In an instant the cloud evaporated. Tim found himself at the edge of the fire. He felt the heat of the flames.

The interior of the bus was alight. A large hole had melted in its bodywork and molten metal was dripping down from the sides like wax. Tim could make out the floor and the bulge of the axle differential beneath it.

De Loudéac turned, screaming. He ran at Sebastian. Tim sped between them, the flashlight gripped in both hands. As de Loudéac reached him, he swung the flashlight at him with all his might. It hit the alchemist a glancing blow on the shoulder, sliced upwards and split open the skin of his cheek. The shock of the impact coursed down Tim's arms.

With one swipe of his arm, de Loudéac thrust Tim to the ground. He fell on his back, his head hitting the earth, mercifully just missing a large stone. The flashlight, his only weapon, flew from his hand. The alchemist drew back his foot to kick him. Tim hunched up, readying himself for the blow, but, instead, de Loudéac seemed to lift off the ground then stagger to one side. In his place stood Pip, a sharp rock in her hand. She reached down and helped Tim up.

"Nice going, sis!" Tim exclaimed, re-arming himself with the Maglite.

Pip made no reply. She was staring in the direction of the bus.

Sebastian was standing up now, the T raised above his head. He had stopped chanting.

Through the hole in the side of the bus, something was moving, thrashing its arms about, moaning deeply.

Behind him, Tim heard a rustling and spun round. De Loudéac had got to his feet, but, instead of attacking, he was rapidly shrinking in size, his black cape looking as if it were sticking to his arms. In a few seconds, he was transformed into a black bird no bigger than a sparrow.

Tim brought the flashlight up over his head to bring it smashing down on the bird, yet he was too slow. It took to the wing and, with a darting flight, disappeared into the blackness of the trees.

Pip grabbed Tim's wrist, her nails hurting him even through the thickness of his sweatshirt.

Against a backdrop of oily flames and the dense smoke of burning plastic and rubber, a creature was making for the hole in the bus. It moved clumsily. Tim thought of how a chimpanzee walked, its arms hanging down by its sides and swinging back and forth.

Sebastian pointed the T at the bus, saying in a loud voice, "In the name of Our Lord, Jesus Christ, I cast you into the outer darkness, where everlasting ruin awaits you and your abettor . . ."

It came on, stumbling out of the vehicle.

"Ay caramba . . ." was all Tim could say.

The homunculus was not as big as he had expected, standing not more than a meter and a half high. It slumped forward as it walked, each step planted heavily on the ground.

As it advanced towards the light of the fire, its appearance became increasingly grotesque and bizarre. One foot was marginally larger than the other. The arms were short but ended in hands that were disproportionately large for them. It seemed to have no sexual organs at all, its groin smooth like that of a child's doll.

Ten steps from Sebastian, it halted, rocking gently to and fro.

"It's not used to walking," Tim said under his breath.

Pip was not paying him any attention. She could not help staring at the beast.

"Look at its hair."

The skin of the homunculus was dark brown and

covered with a fine fur. The hair on its head was blond — Siamese cat blond.

Slowly, like a short-sighted person, it gazed from right to left.

"Oh, God!" Pip muttered. "It has my eyes."

It was then that the homunculus caught sight of Sebastian and launched itself at him. It lurched towards him, its arms outspread, its huge hands fingering the air as if hoping to ensnare him.

Sebastian waited until the last moment, then, like a matador facing a charging bull, he stepped aside. The homunculus pitched forward into the fire, its arms thrashing into the glowing embers, its feet drumming on the earth. As the flames took hold of its flesh, it yapped like a small dog, the tissues shriveling and contorting, melting and dripping into the embers. The air filled with the pungent, poisonous smell of burning phosphorus. In less than a minute, the fire had consumed it.

"It is done," Sebastian announced in a satisfied voice.

"What about de Loudéac?" Tim asked. "He got away. I saw him fly off. Hadn't we better go after him . . ."

"Ultimately, de Loudéac shall be defeated," Sebastian said quietly. "The time will come when he will be conquered. Yet evil itself cannot be eradicated. So long as there is goodness, there must be evil; for everything that exists in nature, there must be an opposite. For there to be light, there must be darkness."

Feeling in his pocket, Sebastian produced a small

glass rod and tapped it against a stone by the fire. The air filled with a high-pitched droning. Pip and Tim felt the soil beneath their feet vibrate momentarily.

Gradually, the sound petered away. Simultaneously, the fire died down, the embers changing into a pile of smoldering ash. The suspension of the bus creaked and the door opened again, a figure shuffling out. From beneath the chassis appeared something moving forward on its belly.

"Hey, dude! What's goin' down?"

It was Splice. Beside him, getting to his feet and shaking dried leaves off himself, was Woof. When he saw Tim, his tail began to wag feebly.

Over the rim of the quarry, a new moon hung in the sky like a silver eyelash.

Of Sebastian, there was no sign.

The sunlight cut through the holes in the slates of the coach-house roof, ending in bright spots on the flagstones. Tim and Pip stood in the center of the floor and looked around. On the walls were the wooden hooks and trees where once had hung bridles, whips, nosebags and reins. A row of metal rings showed where once the horses had been tethered as they were made ready to pull a coach or cart. Cobwebs hung like dusty curtains from the bars of a rusty iron hay basket. From the side of one of the old barrels stacked in the corner grew a bracket fungus.

A swallow veered in through a broken window, saw

them standing there, executed a sharp, midair swerve and flew out again.

"Funny to think they spend the winter in Africa," Pip remarked. She glanced up at the semicircular cup of mud glued to one of the joists of the floor above. "By Christmas," she mused, "those chicks will have seen hippos and zebras and giraffes . . ."

Tim scuffed his foot against the flagstones.

"You think we'll see him again?" he asked.

Pip shrugged.

"I suppose it did all really happen, didn't it?" he continued.

"Yes," his sister replied.

"Yes," Tim repeated, "it did."

He looked at his father's Maglite where he had left it the night before, on a shelf in the coach house. The glass was shattered, the bulb broken and the shaft was so badly dented he could not get the last three batteries out.

"You'd better buy him another one."

"Right," Tim agreed.

"Before he finds that one missing."

"He'll think it got misplaced in the move," Tim said hopefully.

Leaving the coach house, they walked across the field. Where they had gone the night before, the grass was bent. They reached the pool. Long strands of toad's spawn were laced across some filaments of waterweed.

"You know something," Tim said, "we never got to fly."

"Fly?" Pip repeated.

"We never got any flying ointment."

Pip laughed quietly and replied, "Maybe next time . . ."

"If there is a next time," Tim answered. He looked across at the Garden of Eden and the river beyond it. "I'm going fishing," he decided. "What're you going to do for the rest of the summer, sis?"

Sebastian's battle against the dark side of alchemy continues in

# Soul Stealer

the second book about the alchemist's son.

This time the danger comes from a new and unexpected source. Someone possesses Gerbert d'Aurrillac's book of spells — and intends to use it to deadly effect. Tim, Pip, and Sebastian must stop this force of evil, for the fate of the human race may hang in the balance.

If someone steals your bicycle, you buy another.

But what if they steal your soul . . . ?

To be published Spring 2005

**Martin Booth** was born in England and lived in Hong Kong and, for a short time, in Africa until he was twenty, when he became a student in London. Well-known in the United Kingdom as a novelist and a nonfiction writer, as well as a writer of films and television documentaries, he was nominated for the Booker Prize for his novel *The Industry of Souls*.